REUNION AT OLAN

by
Larry Ivkovich

PROLOGUE

Set Perl ~

The Cycle of Merat

The dead and dying were scattered everywhere. Behind Set Perl, fields once pristine with gardens and meadows of flowering zerain were covered with the quickly bloating corpses of opposing armies. The Olanide Troopers and members of the Perliox Ascendancy lay twisted or crumpled together in the final, frozen throes of the ultimate sacrifice. The stench of death hung over the battlefield like a shroud. For those fallen in this bloody confrontation, the Battle of Set Perl was over at last.

The Healer searched among the bodies, looking for those he could save or, at least, comfort. Dressed in leather and chain-mail armor, he looked like any Olanide soldier, save for the red Healer's star sewed on his helm.

Two Olanide Troopers flanked him, watching his back for any Perliox survivors left strong enough or crazed enough who might still mount an assault. The enemy was infamous for suicide attacks, their fanatical onslaughts sometimes completely overrunning any opposition, no matter the cost to themselves.

Devils, the Healer thought, cradling his own

withered left arm to his side. He shifted his wandering gaze to the distant mountains, their snow-capped peaks pointing to the heavens. *That's where the barbarians will run. At last we have finally put them to flight.*

The clear blue sky above the Healer belied the misery on the ground below it. The rich, undulating countryside of Glimmerlaan prefecture lay scarred by flame and sword. The treeline around the city of Perl lay flattened in spots by the great catapults and archery towers that had been dragged through it. Part of the Set itself was afire, the ancient citadel spouting black smoke, though it seemed now to be under control.

Feersah is helping to contain that, the Healer thought of his fiery comrade. *Our Sister of the Flame.* Groups of Olanide Troopers and cavalry took up strategic positions around the Set perimeter and outer boundaries of the battlefield.

They not only had to guard against the Perliox but also that of the dark magic of the Ascendancy's ruling Animists who still could pose a threat.

Aye, the Healer could sense it--the tingling on his skin, the thick, ashy quality of the air he breathed. He was a Gifted One and though he was no farsenser like his comrade Marcus or seer like group-leader Wing-Ma,

4

he could, nevertheless, feel the unnatural crackling of the space surrounding the battlefield. It was a space still interwoven with the slowly dissipating wizardry used by the Animists and the Olanides' Priest-Mages against each other in this terrible conflict.

An afterspell, he thought. *The final remnants of the magickings wrought here.*

He brought his reluctant gaze back to the killing field. Though the long battle (and hopefully the war) was over, the suffering remained. The Perliox forces had been broken and driven from the blood-soaked battlefield. The enemy had been that close to victory. The Healer thanked the Almighty One the Olanide rear guard had rallied to hold the low ground. His own company of Gifted Ones had helped to turn the tide as had First Paladin Dantol's sky-ships, which had miraculously appeared at the end to help rout the enemy by raining fire and stone upon them from their winged crafts.

Yet, this could very well be the worst of it, he knew--this final result of carnage and suffering. The other members of his Gifted company, outdwellers like himself, had enlisted to fight for the Olanides; they had the easy part--all most of them had to do was to wage war using their special powers, moving on quickly to the next battle, the next engagement. He and the many non-Gifted men and women who made up the medical troop saw the consequences of such war more closely, had to tend to whoever had survived the bloodletting, to give relief and show mercy where needed.

He cocked his head as if listening. The feel of magic, the afterspell, was most strong here...

A groan diverted his attention. There! One lay among the torn and battered corpses that needed his help. He knelt, looking into the blood-red eyes of a young Perliox soldier. Pink froth bubbled at the enemy's mouth; his body shook in the agony of dying. The sharp-edged, molded armor he wore had not been able to protect him in the end.

He is one of the hated enemy, the Healer thought, the bile rising in his throat. *And yet...*

"What are you doing, Gifted One?" one of his guards barked, anger edging his voice. His uniform was spattered with blood, his helm broken, his sword nicked and scratched. Contempt filled his words--the Gifted Ones weren't loved by all, no matter the good they did. Those who were different were always suspect to some, especially those granted powers from beyond the world of men. "Leave that scum! There are plenty of our own people who need your unnatural magic more than this piece of Perliox dung."

"He's just a boy," the Healer replied without taking his eyes off the Perliox who was not much younger than himself. But such a boy! Like all of his race, the young trooper's dark-skinned face was covered with ritual tattoos, his features primitive and bestial. His broad, thick body was bleeding from a myriad of wounds. *It's a wonder he's still alive,* the Healer marveled. *He's the enemy but I can't let him die. I must take his pain into myself. I've sworn to use my Gift to help all others, no matter who or what they are.*

He knelt down beside the boy, fighting back his own revulsion at his closeness to the barbarian. He removed his glove and placed his shaking good hand on the Perliox's bloody chest, then moved his forehead towards the boy's own brow. The Healer's medicine was not that of salves, splints and stitches. His special power was one of the mind and spirit and of the accompanying aura that surrounded all living things. He had to touch those who suffered in this intimate manner in order for his "magic" to work. It had been so since he had reached the age of twelve turnings. It was the way of all Gifted

Ones.

Most thought those who were Gifted were born with their special talents, their blood being different, allowing their minds and bodies to become conduits for their abilities when reaching that particular age. Others postulated the ancient Gods of the Imperium had singled them out as special or to be cursed for some infraction done in a previous incarnation. Others thought they were demons, to be shunned at any cost.

At any rate, the Healer and the six others of his Gifted company had been recruited for this war--to add their almost supernatural abilities to the cause of the Olanides--to drive the demon Perliox from Glimmerlaan prefecture forever. But that didn't mean he would ignore any who were in pain.

A strangling cry brought him up short. He whirled to see one of his guards stumbling backwards, clawing at an arrow protruding from his throat. The trooper fell, limbs thrashing, blood spurting from beneath his helm's collar. His body flopped among the dead littering the field.

"No!" Instinctively, the Healer rose to his feet and reached out for the injured trooper.

"Stay down!" shouted the second guard, pushing

him back toward the ground. The Healer knelt again, sudden fear coursing through him. They were under attack! A Perliox guard was rising to his feet only a few arms' lengths away; an already standing second was notching another arrow into his bow. They had been pretending to be dead, to surprise any unsuspecting Olanides in some last, desperate attack.

He looked around wildly for a weapon; he and the other healers were forbidden to carry arms despite their presence in combat. Their chain-mail armor and hard leather helms would protect them only so much. *Insane tradition!* he raged. *Now we're helpless!*

In the distance, some of the mounted Olanide troopers had spotted the Perliox and were racing toward them. *They'll never get here in time despite their fast mounts,* the Healer thought. He berated his own stupidity and that of his guards. *How can we not have not foreseen this? Are we so confident to forget the enemy's insidious tactics?*

The surviving trooper had taken a defensive stance, his sword drawn and at the ready as the Perliox Guard advanced, his own weapon flashing. The second Perliox, the one with the bow, stood watching as if he didn't care. He had discarded his helm, his long, braided hair flowing out over his armored back and shoulders. His piercing eyes burned with hatred out of a gaudily tattooed face.

They know they can't win, the Healer reasoned. *But they'll take as many of us with them as they can.*

Across the battlefield, the Healer could see more of the Perliox rising like wraiths from their graves. They too had begun attacking other members of the medical troop and their guards.

"Cowards!" the Healer shouted as his hand closed around the pommel of a discarded sword. "We're here to help! You monsters... Aaagghhhhhh!" A burning pain sliced through him. As if he were watching someone else, he saw the point of a sword protruding through his poorly armored stomach. The blade retracted and the Healer fell. *No,* he thought, covering his bleeding wound with his hand, his body convulsing in pain. *No...* He couldn't feel his legs; his back...

He turned his head to see the young Perliox he had wanted to help leaning up on one elbow, the other hand holding his freshly bloodied sword. "<u>You</u> are the cowards," the boy whispered hoarsely. "<u>You</u> are the monsters..." His eyes glazed over then and he fell back to the ground.

"Bortrum!"

The Healer turned the opposite way at the sound of his name. Thank the Almighty One, his second guard had finished off his attacker. The horsemen were closer yet still too far away. But the one who had called to him and was rushing to his aid was very near--a woman, her silken-clad body surrounded by an aura of shimmering heat and bright light, who fought her way through other attacking Perliox with fiery blasts of flame that leapt from her fingertips. Sword-wielding Perliox ran to meet her charge and were engulfed in writhing tendrils of fire. Screaming, they dropped their weapons and fell flailing to the ground.

Feersah, the Healer thought. *How did she get here so quickly? How...?* Ah, above him, there--diving from the sky like a giant bird of prey to help the others under attack. Another of his company, Thomas of Earth and Sky... he had brought Feersah.

The First Healer's head swam and he started to tremble with cold. The numbness in his legs was complete, the pain in his back and stomach was excruciating. He felt his life flowing out of him as he gasped for breath. His weakness and curse--to be able to heal all others of external injuries and sickness but not himself--slapped him in the face with its cruel irony. First his arm, shrunken and useless since birth. And now this. He would rather die...

His guard charged the Perliox archer. The enemy calmly raised his free hand... The trooper jerked as if struck; his feet left the ground as his body was thrown into the air by some invisible force. He landed a distance away and moved no more.

A... a magicking! the Healer realized. *This one is an Animist!*

He watched in horror as the Perliox magician slowly turned. He raised his bow and aimed his arrow at Feersah who was close enough now that the Healer could feel her rushing heat. *Surely,* the Healer thought. *Surely Feersah will simply burn or melt that.* A sudden glint of light manifested... the arrowhead was flickering as if it was there yet not there. *No...*

His fiery colleague pointed her hands to launch the pillars of fire that were her Gift. "No." the Healer croaked weakly. "Feersah, get back! The arrow is bespelled!"

Too late as the glinting metal shaft was released. Feersah stumbled as if she had tripped; she clutched at her chest. The Healer watched in horror as, despite the light that surrounded her, Feersah's eyes widened in surprise. She hobbled a few more steps as that same light around her dimmed. She fell, her body sparking and twitching, then finally lay still, yet another corpse added to the pile.

By the Imperium, the Healer thought in anguish. *How has this happened?*

"We will be victorious but at a great and terrible price," Wing-Ma had said to him and the rest of the Seven before they joined the battle. The Gifted seer's words echoed in the First Healer's head, their leader never one to elaborate on his predictions of the future. They were either twisted and mysterious or so simple-seeming that the greater meanings behind them were rarely evident. But seeing Feersah killed so brutally and lying here now close to his own death, the First Healer knew what the Blind One meant at last.

The Animist approached the Healer then and stood over him like a monstrous devil, his frightening stare boring into his. The Perliox raised his hand but, at that moment, a crooked smile spread across his scarified face. He threw his bow down and drew his sword as if the First Healer wasn't worthy of the Animist's magic.

The Healer returned his gaze, struggling not to

look away, not wanting to die groveling and pleading, desiring some honor and dignity here at the end. His mind shifted then, bringing up a picture of another...

Aermisiny. Yes. If only things had been different between him and Aermisiny, if only he had told the Gifted young beauty how he felt about her. He knew now that would be his biggest regret. The Animist pulled his arm back to deliver the final blow...

A rushing of air, a soft shushing sound...

The Animist jerked his head to look upward. Something big fell on him from above, something man-shaped with wings.

Ah, Thomas, the Healer named Bortrum thought sadly, his lifeforce ebbing away. *You are too late. Too late...* He closed his eyes and drifted into darkness.

ℬ

KAILENE

Set Olan

The Cycle of Qua ~

Forty Turnings After

By the Sacred Seven, I pray all is in readiness.

Kailene stood on the siege wall, looking outward toward the defense perimeter surrounding Set Olan. She chewed her lower lip in worried concentration, arms folded at her breasts.

Despite the warding enchantments cast by the Priest-Mage, added defense precautions and security arrangements set up for the Galan-Hai/Shawn-Ryn peace conference, she still felt uneasy. Of course it was Kailene's job to worry, no matter how secure things might seem. She hadn't gotten so far in life so quickly by not trusting her instincts.

Ayo, she whispered softly in her mind as she closed her eyes. *Rowt. Show me.* Her Inner Eye flickered as scenes of the Set's outlying borders coalesced in her mind like images glimpsed through a lens-scope. Her guard-hounds' farsensing abilities and empathic bonding with her allowed Kailene to envision what they saw.

The countryside surrounding Set Olan was some of the most beautiful in Glimmerlaan prefecture. Here, within the rocky borderlands of the northern Olan mountains, productive farmland existed next to lush greenwood and shimmering wetlands; meadows of golden zerain flowed into fruit orchards and grazing tracts. The walled city of Olan (renowned for its eclectic architectural styles and rich artistic traditions) surrounded the Set in a perfect circle. Its churches and monuments were famous for their detailed representational tributes to the Olanides' supreme deity, the Pantocrator--the Almighty One--and the lesser gods of the Imperium.

A series of small lakes and manicured gardens encircled the hilltop Set and its double-moated causeway. In the far distance at the city's fringes, smoke from the fabric mills, forging kilns, metal-working and glass-making furnaces of Olan City's new industrial district spiraled upward into the sky. Yet, Kailene ignored all of that. Such beauty and workmanship could be deceptive and hide any number of dangers.

But not today on Frenten's Eve, it seemed. The hounds' sendings showed nothing untoward within this peaceful setting. *Good, my strong boys,* she thought-sent in return. *Continue your patrols and I'll see you soon.* A shiver within her Eye made her smile--a happy mental obeisance sounded from both Ayo and Rowt, the hounds anxious to serve and please their mistress.

"Marshal Kailene!"

Kailene turned to see her second, Eleanor, approaching. "Extra guards and troopers are in position at the rear battlements as you requested," Eleanor said formally.

Kailene smiled at Eleanor's confident look and proud manner. Kailene wished she could be as calm and relaxed as her second, Eleanor always the more self-assured, even in their Knight-Warden training. Sometimes she wondered how it was that she had been promoted to Marshal rather than her second.

"*Marshal* Kailene, is it?" Kailene teased under her breath, knowing in public all protocol was to be observed. Even so, the title was still new and unfamiliar-sounding to her, though she had earned it.

Eleanor's angled face smirked under short blond hair, her green eyes flashing. "The walls have ears, Kai, do they not?" Eleanor said. "What of Rowt and Ayo then? Any news from our boys?"

Kailene shook her head. "Only the good kind. The boys are well."

"But you're nervous and concerned anyway. As usual."

How can I not be? A sigh. "Walk with me."

Kailene turned and, accompanied by Eleanor, strode briskly along the siege wall's upper rampart. Her second--tall, fair and big-boned and Kailene--shorter (though not by much), lean and dark nodded to the armored paladins on duty.

She sensed their eyes boring into her despite their strict military bearing. The tight, furred leathers she wore for warmth in the autumnal season's chill hugged her lean, sinewy body. Even her long, black, cloak couldn't conceal her exotic sensuality. Her dark brown skin marked her as an indigene of the southernmost border prefectures. She felt the braid that pulled her black hair tightly against her scalp and trailed down her back move sinuously with each step she took as if it had a life of its own.

Out of strict habit, she fingered the pommel of her belted sword and deftly checked her hidden forearm dagger. A soft chuckle sounded from Eleanor. "It's not just your beauty, Kai, that pulls such hardened gazes after you." She paused, her voice lowered a notch as if imitating a member of the Set's paladin guard. "How could the Bishop-Prefect have 'scripted a black Ofrikane as Set Olan's newest Marshal--and one so young and inexperienced at that? And a female as well! What was

19

the old man thinking? Is he bedding her? Has the Council approved such an extraordinary move? And what did the lay priests say? Were the Gods angry at such a break in tradition?" She threw her blond head back and laughed, a rich, hearty sound.

Kailene managed a reluctant chuckle. "Yes, Percin doesn't make it easy, does he? Most of the Olanides are at least civil."

"The opinion of the First Paladin means nothing, Kai," Eleanor said. "He's simply envious and afraid. This is our first watch but we have served before this, fought in small skirmishes, mediated border disputes, helped victims of floods and quakes..."

"Scrubbed privies, mucked out stalls..."

"We were trained by the best Knight-Wardens in the Imperium," Eleanor said, gesturing broadly. "And the Bishop-Prefect has the sense to know what that means despite the fact your skin is darker than his or you come from a border prefecture. And with you at our lead, we'll protect the Set and its conference with every skill we possess, the Sacred Seven willing. The Council and the priests be damned! I mean, it's not like we're going to be attacked by the Perliox!"

Kailene winced at the sound of that ancient foe.

The Perliox had been defeated and exiled forty turnings past. These were new times now, with new enemies. It was hers and Eleanor's time. And perhaps with the Bishop-Prefect's forward-seeing ways, others of less fortunate circumstances could rise to a better station in life like she had done.

"Aye, thanks, Eleanor. I appreciate your trust and confidence." She smiled at her old friend. Despite their differences, she and Eleanor had been lovers once, having gone through Knight-Warden training together. Now as comrades and fellow guardians of the Set, they knew each other intimately. Eleanor was right but Kailene was the Marshall, after all. In the end, this watch at Set Olan was her responsibility no matter what happened.

A pause. *And then there's this... this reunion?* She sighed then as they descended the rock-hewn stairs to the first-level bailey. She did question the Prefect's judgment in that--to schedule two such events at the same time within the Set's walls. On Frenten's Eve, no less! Security was tight enough as it was. She and her personal guard were already stretched to the limit.

"Eleanor, go oversee the preparations at the inner front gate and catch up with the others of our guard." A sigh. "I'll see to the other arrangements personally."

Eleanor cocked her head to one side. "The merchants?"

"Yes! A bunch of greedy, old tradesmen coming together for their seasonal gathering. How sweet." She snorted. "I'd best get down there. Perhaps they need their bread softened with milk for their toothless gums!"

BORTRUM

"The Galan-Hai delegates have arrived," Marcus said softly, eyelids fluttering in his round, fat face. "And the Shawn-Ryn are late, as usual."

"Not being a good thing to angering one's fellow delegates," Solana said, crossing her long and still-shapely legs. "Especially if they being your enemies, heya?"

Marcus laughed, his huge body quivering as the film over his eyes cleared. "There will never be peace between those two warring states, my dear lady. Too much history and blood."

"Can you farsee such an outcome?" Thomas asked softly. He stood by a heavily curtained window, his floor-length, voluminous cloak of dark fabric wrapped securely around his tall frame.

Marcus pursed his lips. "No," he said, easing back into the stack of cushions supporting his bulk. "Future paths are not open to me. If Wing-Ma were still with us, he would know. But common sense dictates..."

"Forget them," Aermisiny chimed in, her voice high and girlish despite her age. She raised a goblet of wine in a frail, delicate hand. "We're not here for politics, surely. The Imperium's problems can do without us for a while. A joyous Frenten's Eve to you all!"

"Yes," Thomas added, holding up his own goblet. "And to another season of living."

"Aye," Bortrum joined in, smiling broadly at his old friends. He pointed to his shriveled legs and stump of a left arm. "If you call this living!"

A chorus of laughter followed as goblets clinked around the circular dining table. Aermisiny gently squeezed Bortrum's good arm, her eyes smiling. Bortrum eased back in his chair, studying his four old comrades-in-arms.

This particular room was normally reserved for gatherings that were much less formal in nature--more for personal meetings and celebrations. Still, the high ceilings, exquisite paintings, tapestries and ceramics that graced the walls, tables and sideboards were of the finest taste. The wooden floors, mantels and trim were polished till they shone; candles and the newly invented light-orbs shed a steady, calming glow throughout; spears, shields and battle axes were hung strategically to remind guests that Set Olan was still a functioning temple-fortress. Despite the lesser importance of this chamber, the Bishop-Prefect didn't believe in slighting any of his guests.

The remains of Bortrum's left arm throbbed as usual. He ignored it as he had done all of his life. Instead, he focused on those who were left of his old company--and a very special company they had been. They had helped the Bishop-Prefect once, so long ago when the Set's ruler had been a mere First Paladin (though a strong one!). And now they had returned at the religious leader's invitation, albeit older and not so ready to do battle.

Truly, he thought with a grim smile. *Most of us are still here and does this take me back! Let's hope there are more reunions to come.*

Marcus raised his eyebrows. "Someone's approaching," he said and then, with a malicious smile, "It's that dark sweetmeat of a Marshal. Oh my, what I wouldn't do to..."

"You're disgusting," Aermisiny chided.

Solana rolled her almond-shaped eyes. "As being usual, heya? Besides, I seeing her first."

"Ah hah!"

"Age hasn't mellowed either of you at all, has it?" Aermisiny scolded. "I feel sorry for your poor wife,

Marcus."

"My 'poor wife' cares not a whit!" Marcus shook his head. "Mellowing, my lovely Aermisiny, would be the death of me!"

There was a tolling knock on the doors.

ಲ

KAILENE

Kailene knocked once on the dining hall doors, the elaborate sounders ringing like bells. She walked in and stopped, turning her critical gaze to the five individuals awaiting within.

Sitting around the dining table near the hearth were the five merchants. Actually, Kailene noted, only four sat--the fifth, a tall cloaked hunchback, stood back away from the others.

"Good midday, noble lords and ladies," she announced to the room with a short bow, all the while taking note of the five elders facing her. *Merchants,* she thought in disgust, remembering how her own family had been fleeced by such as these when she was a girl. They had been left destitute until her father had found favor with their prefecture's ruling family. *Robbers of the poor.*

She made a quick reassessment of each since she had only perfunctorily greeted them upon their arrival--a woman of about fifty-odd winter seasons, hardly larger than a small child, sat dressed in peasant shirt and blue, sashed pants, her tiny feet encased in black slippers. Her long white hair was done up in a peak with a long tail of it hanging down to her shoulders.

An enormously fat man, garbed in a long, belted white robe that covered his massive frame, sat next to her on a wide bench, covered in pillows. His age was indeterminate but Kailene guessed he might be older than any of the others. He was hairless and quite repulsive-looking yet he returned Kailene's gaze with more than a passing interest. In fact, Kailene noted with amused distaste, he winked at her.

Seated at his left was another female, this one dressed in tight and very fashionable quant-skin vest-coat, leggings, boots and gloves. Though seemingly as old as the small woman, this one was very tall and slender. Short black and gray-streaked hair crowned her angled face. Her eyes slanted upward in a face with skin the color of young lemon fruit, marking her as an inhabitant of the Tapa isles, perhaps. Kailene's gaze lingered on the woman. She had noticed her briefly when these five had arrived but now blinked, surprised at her ageless beauty. The woman smiled.

Kailene forced her stare away from the woman and looked behind the table where the tall, completely cloaked hunchback stood. Kailene guessed him to be in his sixties, yet he seemed fit, his gray hair long and tied in a tail behind his back. If not for the hump on his back, outlined through the cloak, he would have been quite fetching for a man. He raised his goblet to her in a mock salute.

The last merchant, seated at the table, was a surprise. He was Ofrikane. Once he may have been handsome with those strong features and high cheekbones but his broken body had shrunk him into a sadly crippled state. A specially designed set of crutches leaned against his chair, one outfitted with an elaborate set of straps and bindings, no doubt for his wasted upper limb. She wondered if he had been born in such a state.

"Greetings, sister," he said in a clear, rich voice that belied his physical appearance. "How refreshing to meet a fellow countryman so far from home and one in such a prominent position as well. It is most gratifying. I am Bortrum, once of Semilate prefecture."

"Ah! I know Semilate well--my stepmother was born there."

A pleased smile answered her remark. "We must talk then later, if you have the time. I would be interested in any recent news of home." He then gestured to each of his companions in turn as he introduced them.

"And, again, I'm Kailene, Marshal of Set Olan,"

she said afterwards. "I'm sorry I wasn't able to greet you properly when you arrived. Set Olan hosts another gathering besides yours and my time has been sorely taken up."

"We understand." Bortrum smiled, his dark brown face lighting up (*Aye,* Kailene thought with approval. *Handsome once, indeed*). "Our needs are few and we will be here only another day or two at the behest and convenience of the Bishop-Prefect. We will pose no problem for you and will not interfere in the other gathering, I assure you. Please go about your business."

Kailene bowed and then paused. A tingling sensation crawled over the skin between her eyes. She turned toward Marcus, the fat merchant, and took a step toward the table. "You are a farsenser," she said, frowning at the man, a moment of vague uneasiness washing over her. A merchant <u>and</u> a Gifted One! A dangerous combination. Why hadn't she been informed?

"Ah, well... I..."

"You feeling that?" The tall woman named Solana speared Kailene with a heated gaze. Kailene felt a wriggling warmth trickle down her spine. It was not unpleasant. "You being sensitive to picking up on

Marcus' lecherous probing. Perhaps even possessing an Inner Eye, heya?"

"Solana! I was not..." Marcus sputtered.

Kailene nodded, returning Solana's own probing look. "I'm not Gifted, but I do have some talents." No sense in pretending, it seemed--these individuals were apparently familiar with farsensing bonding techniques developed by the Imperium's Beastmasters long ago.

"As the Marshal of Set Olan would," Bortrum broke in with approval.

"My father was a liege lord to the Prince-Prefect of Atmium prefecture," Kailene said. "He was the Master Beastman; he and his assistants trained the castle's horses, falcons and hounds."

"And you were one such assistant?" Bortrum asked.

"Aye and a Knight-Warden-in-training," She said proudly, remembering her family's approval. "Females are treated more equally in Atmium than in other parts of the Imperium. But more so, I was found to be thought-sensitive and could bond with the animals to certain degrees and communicate through their own farsensing. Two such hounds are my dear comrades and fellow wardens. They patrol the outer borders here. We have been assigned to Set Olan for three moons now having been called here to help oversee the preparations for the peace conference."

"Your father and mother must be very proud of you."

Kailene nodded, a bittersweet smile on her lips. "And so my father told me--before he died. I never knew my real mother though my stepmother still lives."

"I grieve for your loss, sister," Bortrum said, his eyes shining with compassion. "But you need not fear Marcus' prying into affairs not of our concern. We know of the conference and will respect all security measures."

Kailene bowed again and then said to Bortrum, "Very good, noble sir. I'll hold you to that but since the Bishop-Prefect has invited you here and your records-of-commerce are spotless, there should be no problem. In the meantime, His Grace wishes you all to join him this evening for refreshment. Afterwards, Frenten's Eve services will be held in the Nave of the Pantocrator that you are welcome to attend. This may be his grace's last free time to see you before the conference begins tomorrow. A paladin will arrive at dusk to escort you to the dining hall. Good midday to you all."

And good riddance. Yet, the one called Bortrum

seemed kind enough. Perhaps not all merchants were the same. Kailene turned then to leave and swore, with a reluctant thrill, she could feel Solana's piercing eyes following her.

༄

BORTRUM

"It is good to see you again, Your Grace." Bortrum bowed as much as his misshapen body would allow him within the confines of the chair he sat in.

The Bishop-Prefect, once Bortrum's friend and comrade and one-time supporter of the Gifted Ones, took the Ofrikane's good hand warmly in both of his. "As it is to see you, Bortrum," he said, his voice a hoarse whisper. Bortrum could see a portion of a scar on the leader's neck revealed beneath his vestment collar. "It has been too long. I am so pleased. And, I beg you, at least for this evening, call me Dantol as you did in our younger, more foolish days."

"Ah, but what days they were!" Bortrum replied with a laugh.

Bortrum and his comrades had dressed in their best regalia to meet with the man who had once sponsored and defended them. Yet, even in his embroidered tunic and the loose breeches Aermisiny had woven for him, Bortrum still felt shabby and out-of-place within the Bishop-Prefect's opulent Great Hall.

In place of torches, light-orbs cast a mock luminesce throughout the chamber. Coats-of-arms of the prefectures of the Imperium graced the walls alongside banners, tapestries and paintings of the Bishop-Prefect's predecessors. The table and chairs were meticulously carved in oak and *traven*-wood, glinting in the light with gold-leaf highlights.

He blinked at the irony. Even though Dantol stood in front of him, aged like them all yet still vigorous and fit and dressed in his religious finery, the silver skullcap of his office resting comfortably on his head, even though Bortrum and his company had helped put the Bishop-Prefect on the throne, even though the Sacred Ones had fought so many turnings ago to rid Glimmerlaan prefecture of the tyranny and cruelty of the barbarian Perliox--something just didn't feel right.

More than anyone, Bortrum and the others deserved to be here. And yet he and those who were Gifted, who had been blessed with certain special talents, had faded like ghosts into the background of their society--over the seasons their kind had been replaced by other, more "reasonable" or "acceptable" or "normal" personages, methods and ideas.

Sadly, even here times had changed. This was the first time since the Battle of Perl that Bortrum and the other surviving Gifted Ones had visited the royal seat.

Even here, it seemed different, uncomfortable.

He looked at Dantol, the Bishop-Prefect. *Not the same man,* he thought. *On no, as none of us are, are we?* Aermisiny and Marcus had already made their salutations and gone immediately to the elaborately-sculpted sideboards where heaping plates of food and drink awaited them. Aermisiny looked lovely in her blue-and-white over-dress, Marcus as large as ever in a black, sashed robe. The two began eating as if they were starved.

"How does she put away so much food and stay so small?" Dantol asked with an amused expression. "She eats as much as Marcus."

Bortrum chuckled. "More. It is part of her Gift, after all."

The Bishop-Prefect nodded. Bortrum followed his gaze toward Solana. The Tapan Islander was garbed in a floor-length, velvet-spun, purple gown with bell sleeves, helping herself to wine. Thomas stood aloof in a long red cloak, his muscular legs garbed in black hosen, his eyes fixed on the tall graceful woman. "Thomas still hungers for her, I see," Dantol said, shaking his head. "And he continues to hide his Gift, as always."

"Aye," Bortrum acknowledged. "His love for the

strong-willed Solana will never die, I'm afraid, and he has been hounded most of his life for being different. All of our Gifts but his are unseen."

"The troubled one, as always. Well! And how have you fared these past many seasons, my friend? Merchants indeed!"

Bortrum nodded, pursing his lips. "Well enough. We all have carved out lives filled with a certain amount of contentment. Each of us does a fair business in various areas of trade and commerce--Marcus with food imports and exports (though it's a wonder he doesn't eat all of his profits!), Solana with her paintings, Thomas with land stewardship in the Imperium's outer holdings and myself and Aermisiny as partners in the acquiring and selling of ancient books. All of us but Solana and Thomas have families and children." He smiled at the look on Dantol's face. "Aye, aye. Don't look so surprised--Aermisiny and I..."

Dantol raised his eyebrows. "Aermisiny? Children?" A shadow seemed to cloud Dantol's face then, only to be brightened by his smile. "I always thought there was a spark between you two. I remember how she stood by your bedside those long moments when we thought we had lost you. That is good news. I thank the Almighty One again that Thomas was able to bring you off the battlefield in time to save you that day."

Bortrum nodded, looking affectionately toward the small woman while pushing the memory of his crippling injury to the back of his mind. "We have been happy together as strange as it may seem to most people. The outlying districts of the hinterlands have accepted all of us as citizens well enough. And you, Your Grace, er, beg your pardon, Dantol?"

A resigned shrug. "Many things have changed since we drove the Perliox into exile. We have factories now--with the new forging and kilning techniques. Our Master Smithies present new ideas and inventions to us every day. Why, our garrison at Fort Pennit employs motorized vehicles--wagons and carts that run under their own power!" He shook his head. "It is a wonder, this new Industrial Age we dip our toes in, yes, old friend?"

Motorized vehicles? Bortrum agreed reluctantly. The old ways were fast disappearing, he knew, but there were times when he wished events weren't moving so swiftly. The days of the Gifted Ones were numbered as a result.

"The Galan-Hai and Shawn-Ryn are the newest threats to Glimmerlaan prefecture," Dantol continued. "Their war will overtake not only our own territory but all of the Imperium if we don't try to settle this now."

"I know." Bitterness rose in Bortrum then as that hated memory of their past enemy reluctantly returned. "Both are not as barbarous or insidious or clever compared to the Perliox. I warrant you'll be able to settle their differences easily enough."

Dantol sighed, looking away. "Let us hope. Their disputes have already lasted three turnings. They could still pose a serious threat if not stopped. But let us talk of this later." His look became dark and faraway again then as if he recalled some past transgression. "These are troubled times, my friend," he said softly. "Perhaps change is not a bad thing for we Olanides. Or the Imperium."

Bortrum stared, not fully understanding. Dantol waved his hand in a dismissive gesture. "Come!" he said. "A toast from my special brew!"

A dark amber ale was uncorked and poured for each diner by servants who promptly exited the room. Dantol raised his mug. "To old friends," he called out. "And new alliances!"

The ale tasted good and refreshing as Bortrum drained his mug. He licked his lips in satisfaction but then noticed Dantol had not drunk. Instead, the Bishop-Prefect had put his mug down on the table and looked sharply at Bortrum. It was not the look of the friend Bortrum once knew.

At that moment, Bortrum's Gift ignited, warning him of an attack on his bodily humors. The ale... He turned sharply towards his comrades. *Danger,* he thought. *There is danger here.*

His eyes widened in alarm. Suddenly everything had changed--Solana had fallen to the floor as if ill. Thomas was struggling to reach her, his knees buckling. Aermisiny was staggering towards Bortrum, a look of puzzlement and fear written on her face. Marcus was slumped over the table at his seat.

Bortrum felt dizzy; a stinging warmth rushed through his body; his head felt as if it were on fire; his breath came in short, ragged gasps.

"The soporific works exceedingly fast, does it not?" Dantol loomed over him, his figure wavering and indistinct. Bortrum struggled to keep his eyes open.

<u>Drugged!</u> he thought. <u>Why...?</u>

"Did you not think it strange you were all allowed

here at the same time as the peace conference was being held?" Dantol leaned in closer, his eyes glittering with some strange emotion, his lower lip quivering. "Did you not feel that was more than mere coincidence?" He laughed, a hard scratchy sound. "You have slipped... old friend."

"Dantol? What... what are you doing?" The room spun. As Bortrum sunk into darkness, he saw Dantol smiling down on him. He heard the Bishop-Prefect speak again, as if from a great distance. "We have a great wrong to right, Bortrum. Even your Gift won't help you now."

Bortrum watched as, incredibly, the body of the Bishop-Prefect began to change--it flickered and seemed to fall in upon itself, wavering and pulsating. The air around it appeared to curl and bubble. The figure shook with some hideous metamorphosis until the familiar personage that stood before them was no longer that of the Bishop-Prefect.

Then Bortrum knew no more.

ജ

KAILENE

Ayo, where are you? Ayo...? Kailene frowned. Her Inner Eye could not pick up on her guard-hound. Perhaps it was nothing. Ayo may have simply not been casting his farsenses. The dogs could become fatigued by too much mental activity. Still...

Rowt, she called to her second hound. Rowt's happy voice sounded within her mind. *Leave your patrol and find Ayo.* She ran her fingers over the dagger-holster strapped to her left forearm, hoping nothing had happened.

"Anything amiss, honored Marshal?" asked the First Prelate. The short, elaborately coifed and robed priest stood with Kailene. Kailene wrinkled her nose at the man's strong perfume as he added haughtily, "I realize this is your first watch but the Priest-Mage's warding spells should be sufficient to block any intrusions."

Kailene nodded curtly, wishing the First Prelate would go do something else. He reminded her of her first sponsor after she had finished her training, exceedingly vain and prissy. It was a wonder she had gotten anywhere under that one's patronage.

Still, she noticed the man fidgeted, his eyes roving the rooftops of Olan City and beyond as if searching for something. "And you, noble lord," she said, noting his anxiousness. "Anything amiss with you?"

"Ah, no, no." The prelate's hands fluttered like birds. "It is exciting, is it not? To host such an important gathering? I admit to being a shade nervous."

Kailene grunted and turned back then to the business at hand. The Shawn-Ryn peace delegates and their security contingent had finally arrived. They had been escorted through the city and then stopped at the outer moat, the gate lowered in courtesy as they were questioned by the frontline guard. A member of their congregation had been picked as the ceremonial hostage, to remain at the outer gate tower with a corresponding Galan-Hai member until the conference was over.

After passing that first security check, the Shawn-Ryn now approached the inner moat and the Set's main keep. The officials and troopers traveled easily on horseback while their slaves carried boxes and chests of supplies or bore ceremonial banners. Six specially masked, bare chested servants pulled a large, covered wagon in the middle of the procession.

Kailene studied them from the upper rampart as the group of delegates, servants and troopers crossed the inner moat bridge. By custom, the Shawn-Ryn officials wore ceremonial robes complete with intricately sewn facial hoods that covered their entire heads. They were an intensely private race. Their religious doctrine specifically prohibited their faces to be revealed in public outside their prefecture except under certain conditions.

This conference must be anathema to them, Kailene thought distastefully. To force the Shawn-Ryn to be under such scrutiny, especially during Frenten's Eve, a holiday their kind didn't celebrate in any case, showed that the Shawn-Ryn were serious about the conference.

The troopers likewise were clad in visored helms, their armor looking to be more light-weight and flexible then other such garb. Here at the last checkpoint, they would hand over all weapons and banners to the Set's paladin guard per conference precepts.

Kailene looked curiously at the large, decorated wagon. *Gifts for the Galan-Hai and the Bishop-Prefect,* she mused thoughtfully. *But the conveyance is bigger than what we were told it would be.*

The lead trooper halted the procession and formally announced their arrival to the Set guard in a loud, booming voice. All proceeded as ritual at this point--protocol would still be observed. The paladin of the gate cried out in response and ordered the inner gate doors to be opened.

At that moment, a cry reverberated within Kailene's Inner Eye. She blinked in surprise at the intensity of the sound, the pain. It was Ayo but the hound was terrified and hurting. Kailene gasped as blurred images formed inside her mind.

Men and women--dead and stripped of their clothes; the ground soaked with blood; smoke and fire burned and drifted everywhere. Ayo whined, his mental tether to Kailene fading in and out. Ayo! she shouted into the aether. *My boy! What has happened?*

Ayo brought a view of one of the dead closer and sharply into focus. Kailene knew the effort it must be taking on her beloved hound. But she saw... a ring on the corpse's finger... its stylized design...

By the Seven, she thought in horror. *It is the royal sigil of the Shawn-Ryn.* She turned her mental focus to her second hound, trying not to let her thoughts betray her._Rowt! Hurry to Ayo. Here is the way. Tend him!

49

The gate was almost completely opened.

"No!" Kailene shouted, shocked realization rushing through her. "Close the gate! Prelate, sound the alarm!" She ran past the surprised priest and leaped down the stairs three at a time. "Eleanor! Kain!" she cried out to her two nearest personal guards. "They are not the Shawn-Ryn!"

Too late. The troopers at the front of the procession charged the opened gate, using their horses as battering rams to force their way through the group of paladins. Brandishing suddenly-drawn swords and axes, they cut down the surprised guards at the gate entrance. With an ear-splitting cry, the slaves pulling the wagon heaved and dragged the conveyance halfway through the front entrance, smashing into the gate doors and effectively keeping them from closing.

Kailene drew her sword and threw off her cloak as a gong sounded from somewhere behind her. The alarm--the First Prelate wasn't so worthless after all

She hit the courtyard tiles running just as the five members of her personal guard began their own defensive attack. The ringing of flashing steel and the cries of the combatants shattered the air. Behind her, more of the Set's paladins stormed into the courtyard.

These impostors are outnumbered, Kailene thought, parrying a sword thrust by one of the invaders. *What are they trying to do?*

She brought her sword up and around, deflecting her attacker's blade. And then whirled back again to pierce his armor, chest and backbone. Jumping over the falling corpse, Kailene ran toward the gate, seeing her personal guard fighting alongside the Set's paladins.

The foot soldiers of the enemy unleashed a storm of bolts from their crossbows. Kailene ducked behind a statue of one of the Imperium's ancient heroes, others under attack following her course. The bolts exploded upon impact, the deadly projectiles cleaving men in two and breaking stone into rubble. *Explosive weaponry,* she thought frantically. What magic is this? She whirled at a cry from behind--a horse and rider charged her, the rider swinging a battle axe at her head.

Instinct and training kicked in as Kailene dropped and rolled under the deadly blow. She regained her feet as the rider ran his horse past her but whipped around for another pass. Kailene stretched out her mental focus to touch the horse's mind. Her power wasn't much without her hounds to amplify it, but it was enough to confuse the horse. The animal slowed, snorting in fright as its rider screamed at its sudden indecision.

Kailene leaped up and jerked the distracted rider from the horse, knocking him to his back. Her sword found its mark again as she thrust it through her attacker's midsection.

"Kai!"

Kailene looked toward the sound of Eleanor's voice. Her second pointed frantically to the rear of the courtyard where Galan-Hai troopers were now streaming in to join the battle. *Too many,* she thought in alarm. *The courtyard and bailey are too small for so many soldiers. Too crowded...*

She started, her eyes widening, as she looked at the battered wagon. *It's bigger than it should be, the attackers are so few, the crossbow bolts...*

"Eleanor!" she screamed. "Kain! Everyone! Fall back!"

The wagon exploded. Tongues of fire, balls of flaming gas and deadly columns of detritus erupted from it, shattering the inner gate and its supporting ramparts. Men of both forces fell burning as debris of the siege wall itself rained down on the Set's courtyard.

A hot wind plucked Kailene off her feet and tossed her through the air like a doll. She hit something hard and lay still. *No,* she thought, groaning. *I won't let this happen. Not on our first watch!* She struggled to her feet, sword still in hand. Her head flared in pain.

Something fell like rain, spattering against the tiles. *Blood,* she thought, sickened. A severed head, that of the First Prelate, gaped open-mouthed at her only a few steps away.

The inner gate was aflame and in ruins. Most of the attacking forces, their mounts and the Set's paladins were dead, bodies and body parts strewn everywhere. Kailene's stomach roiled, her head spun. She felt blood trickling down the side of her head.

Another explosion rocked in the distance. *The outer gate,* she realized. *They're opening up the Set's defenses for a larger attacking force. The hostage must have hidden a weapon somehow.*

"Kai!" Eleanor ran up to her, blood streaming from a shoulder wound. "Are you all right?"

Kailene turned toward the Set proper. "We've got to get inside. Protect the Bishop-Prefect and the Galan-Hai delegates. Kain? Nestra? The others?"

Eleanor's face turned hard, her eyes fighting back tears of grief and anger. Her broad shoulders slumped. "Gone," she said softly.

"No!" Rage blossomed within Kailene. "Those filthy animals!" She stopped hard. A corpse lay before her and Eleanor--one of the invaders. The facial hood had been ripped from its head. Covered in tattoos, its dark, broad-features stared up at her with lifeless eyes-- red, unblinking eyes.

Kailene felt the bile rise in her throat, heard Eleanor's gasp of disbelief. *Perliox,* she thought in horror. *It's the Perliox.*

&

BORTRUM

He was swimming for his life. Up from a murky bottom of some unknown sea he rose, laboring, struggling with his last reserves of strength.

The small amount of air remaining in his lungs burned; his chest felt as though it would burst. Both arms and legs pumped frantically as he rose upward through the thick, turgid, heavy water. The pressure surrounding his naked body threatened to crush him.

But still he ascended, forcing his way methodically toward the light that rippled overhead through the water's glimmering surface. His limbs propelled him through the water like the dolphs he had seen at play on the Wickert Coast when he was a child. So long ago... his mother, his father... before his Gift had been discovered.

If only he had been older when the plague had struck his village. The Gifted Ones' powers blossomed only at a certain age. He could have saved his parents from the disease. He could have cured them.

He was almost there; the light was just in reach.

His last breath rushed out in a frantic torrent of bubbles, his head flooded with pain. The muscular legs he once knew shook with exhaustion. He was almost there, almost. His grasping, desperate fingers touched the light...

ଙ

"Aaaahhhhhhh!" Bortrum shuddered as air rushed into his lungs. He choked and coughed, turning over on his side to vomit, again and again. He lay on the carpeted floor, stomach roiling, his chair overturned. Pushing himself up on his right elbow and the stump of his ruined arm, he breathed deeply over and over.

He had done it. The poison in his system had been fast and vile. Dontal, no doubt, had been counting on that to overcome all of them quickly. But Bortrum had managed to flush it out of his system, just barely. Realizing what had been happening before he succumbed had enabled that part of his mind that controlled his Gift to wall itself away from the soporific's deadly advance before it had affected him. Had he not acted then, he would not have been able to stave off the soporific's affects. Now he must use his Gift of Healing on the others before it was too late.

He disengaged himself from the chair and started

crawling toward the sideboard. He struggled, pulling himself along agonizingly slowly. He felt weak and drained but he must not falter!

Aermisiny was the closest, She of Brawn and Might. He crawled to his wife's side and felt for her heartbeat at her tiny neck. Still alive, thank the Almighty One. He placed his hand on her chest, his forehead to hers and closed his eyes...

ℒ

It wasn't Dontal but someone else, someone with his face and body...

Bortrum's eyes fluttered open as a mug of cool liquid was placed to his lips. He had faded into unconsciousness again. But this time he awoke sitting in a righted chair, placed there by his friends. "Easy, my love." Aermisiny whispered softly, standing by his side. "You're weak from reviving all of us. Exerting so much of your Gift has taken its toll on you."

Bortrum swallowed the wine gratefully. His wife looked pale and shaky. "All?" he asked. "What of Marcus? I couldn't reach him."

"Yes, all but Marcus." Thomas came into view above him, his face wan from the poison's affect but filled with a determined anger. "He is gone. Dantol must have taken him."

Bortrum gently pushed the mug away. "Taken him? Aye, aye, for his Gift of Farsensing; to use him for whatever purpose this thing posing as our Bishop-Prefect desires."

"Posing?" Thomas asked with a frown. "What do you mean?"

"It wasn't Dantol but some kind of shifter. I saw it changing just before I blacked out."

"Who then?"

"I fell to the effects of the soporific before I could discern any more."

"By the Pantocrator," Aermisiny gasped. "Does this mean this shifter gained access to the Set by trickery or..."

"Or did Dantol allow it in?" Bortrum finished grimly.

"But why? Why would Dantol be betraying us?" Solana paced near the windows, her face twisted in anguished rage. She visibly shivered as if cold. "Why would he be doing this, if true?"

Bortrum sat up straight. "Remember the shifter's toast? 'Here's to old friends and new alliances?' Aye, I fear Dantol may have made a bargain with the enemy, whoever that enemy might be."

"Curse him!" Thomas whirled, his cloak twisting and winding around him in the rush of sudden air. He strode over to Solana, reached out to her then pulled back as the tall woman brought her hands up in a gesture of denial and turned away.

Aermisiny leaned in close. "What enemy? And why all the deception? I can't believe this of him!"

"I don't know. But much time has passed. Who knows how and why any of us could change under certain circumstances? The shifter told me it was no coincidence the five of us are here at the same time as the peace conference."

Sounds of thunder cascaded from outside. The very walls of the dining hall shook, the window glass and chandeliers rattled. A painting fell crashing to the floor. Bortrum started. "By the Almighty One... Thomas, the windows!"

"Locked and bolted from the outside, it seems. As is the door."

Bortrum nodded to his wife. "Stand back," Aermisiny commanded. She took hold of one of the heavy, oaken chairs in her delicate hands and lifted it over her head as easily as if it was a feather. Utilizing her Gift of Strength, she spun around once, twice and on the third time flung the chair at the window so fast and hard it seemed a blur.

The chair broke the thick glass and tore through the wooden casements, lead bindings and locks. From the now-shattered open window, sounds of battle raged. "I not seeing what's happening," Solana said as she stood on her toes to look out. "But a great cloud of smoke be rising from the way of the inner gate. And... and the outer one too, it looking like."

Bortrum clenched his teeth. "The Set is under attack by, I fear, Dantol's 'new alliance.' Thomas..."

The tall man nodded. "Yes," he said. "I will see what is happening." He unclasped his cloak and dropped it to the floor, revealing a pair of large leathery wings sprouting from his bare back. Bat-like in appearance, the pinions' membranes were veined in blue and red, rimmed in smooth, pointed bone.

He climbed to the broken window's wide inner sill and turned around, garbed only now in tight-fitting hosen and sandals, his barrel-chested torso bare. "I'll be back as quickly as I can." He shot a short glance at Solana and then back again. His eyes were filled with sorrow. "We've been here before, my friends."

"Aye," Bortrum nodded. "But we were younger and there were seven of us. Have a care, Thomas. Return as quickly as you can and follow us. We'll head towards the entrance gallery."

Thomas pushed off from the sill and dropped straight down out of sight. A moment later he reappeared, his wings lifting him in graceful motion, his Gift of Flight carrying him through the air towards the courtyard.

"Eeeyah, Bortrum!" Solana cried. "What can four old fools like us doing? We don't even knowing what's happened! And it's being so long..."

"We're Gifted," Aermisiny said softly, her doll-like face hardened with reluctant resolve. "And therefore, we're obliged to help in any way we can."

"I knowing that!" Solana shot back, frustration edging her voice. "I only meaning..."

"We must, at least, see if anyone is injured," Bortrum said gently. He tucked one crutch under his right arm and affixed the other to the ruined left. Taking a breath, he pulled himself to his feet and turned toward his wife. "Thomas said the doors are locked?"

Aermisiny nodded and walked to the dining hall doors. Leaning her slight weight against them, she pushed...

The doors splintered outward, the lock and crossbar shattering. Shouts resounded from the outside corridor as Aermisiny disappeared from view.

Thumping, crashing sounds followed, punctuated by grunts and yells of pain. Solana helped Bortrum to the broken doorway, both of them seeing Aermisiny standing between two fallen Olanide troopers she had evidently overpowered. "They were approaching the dining room," the diminutive Sacred One said, holding up several strands of rope in one hand and a group of chains in the other. "And they were carrying these."

"To be binding us?" Solana turned a puzzled gaze to Bortrum.

"Apparently so."

"I confused. They taking Marcus and then come back to tie us up?"

"Yes, interesting," Bortrum mused. "I wonder if they thought we would still be under the effects of the soporific."

"And," Aermisiny said, laying down the rope and chains. "As big as Marcus is, it wouldn't have been easy to carry him while he was in an unconscious state."

"Time enough to speculate later!" Bortrum

snapped, suddenly irritated and not knowing why. "Let us proceed. And quickly!"

৪৩

THOMAS

Thomas darted among Set Olan's five tower keeps, staying behind the pointed ziggurats' cover and shadow as much as he could. From this height, he could get a broad view of the temple-fortress' grounds but he would be equally at risk of being seen.

His wing muscles moved effortlessly, powering him strongly over the fortress proper. Despite his age and a move to a more "respectful" lifestyle, he had still kept in shape over the years, flying through the lands he held in stewardship to maintain his wings' strength and flexibility. Despite's his Gift's physical drawbacks, it had given him pleasure and power unknown to most and was not to be ignored and left neglected.

He dropped closer--panic and chaos ruled below. The alarm gong sounded frantically. Many of the Set's clerics, prelates and nuns ran in terror. Paladins and assorted supernumeraries seemed to be trying to restore some semblance of order with varied success.

He ascended on a sudden updraft, the cool autumn air swelling his wings' membranes like skim-boat sails and sending a pleasant chill through his body. Circling back, he landed on the narrow top-level walkway of the foremost tower. *No watchman,* he thought, taking a quick look inside the watch-turret's guard room. *That's unusual.*

Then he noticed blood on the floor. He ducked inside the turret to see the Olanide watchman lying dead, the door to the tower interior open. A chill ran through Thomas' body.

Quickly he went back outside and leaned over the tower's short stone rampart. From this hidden vantage point, he could see the inner gate and the courtyard below.

Thomas gasped, but not from the smoke, which spiraled upward over his head and dissipated like writhing serpents. The inner gate lay in flaming ruins; what was left of dozens of bodies sprawled like shards of broken pottery. The courtyard had become an abattoir. More confusion reigned at the outer Set gate and beyond. It looked like the main fortress walls had been breached as well.

Bortrum was right, he thought, his wings trembling in anger. *We* are *under siege.* He thought of Solana then, his anger turning to sadness. He and the Gifted exotic had fought together before--as comrades and... He jerked his head upward. A noise burst like a screeching flock of birds from above...

Two enormous sky-ships, black as night with their own man-made pinions outstretched, dropped from the clouds and descended like malevolent star-demons toward Set Olan.

ॐ

KAILENE

Kailene and Eleanor raced down the stairway to the sub-corridor entrance just as the sky-ships' menacing bulks came into view. "By the Sacred Seven," Eleanor breathed, looking skyward. "What madness is this?"

"Brilliant, calculated madness," Kailene replied, momentarily in awe of the obviously well-planned strategy set forth against them. "They mean to disrupt the conference and capture the Set, at the very least."

Eleanor turned a confused and disbelieving look to her Marshal. "But the Perliox don't have the resources for such ships. How...?"

"They must be in league with another. How else could they have broken the guarding spells of their exile? They must have had help!" Kailene unbolted the door--the lower-level sub-corridors were used mainly for the movement of supplies and trade goods. As Marshal, Kailene possessed a key to most of the Set's primary entrances.

She and her second entered. Outside, the anguished cries of the still-living, the crackling of flames and crashing of mortar and timber were silenced when Kailene reluctantly closed and locked the door behind them.

"In league with who?" Eleanor asked, her voice rising, spittle flying from her mouth. "Who would sanction this cowardly attack?"

"No time for that now. Protecting the Bishop-Prefect and the delegates is our primary concern. There will be more Perliox forces coming from the sky-ships. Of that, I'm certain." She gave Eleanor a hooded glance, her head wound forgotten as she fought the rage within her. "Revenge will have to come later. But I promise you, the others' deaths will be atoned for!" She looked at Eleanor's bleeding shoulder. "How badly...?"

Eleanor waved Kailene's concerns aside, her features set. "I'm fine. Let's just get going!" Kailene gave her second's hand a squeeze and then set off down the dimly lit corridor. Though Kailene grieved the loss of Kain, Nestra and the rest of her guard, she thanked the Sacred Seven that Eleanor still fought by her side.

Eleanor was Kailene's best--that was why she was second in command. And Kailene needed the best now. For within herself, Kailene battled the fear that threatened to engulf her. And the horror. What had gone wrong? Could she have done something differently?

Surely, no one could have been prepared for this!

No, she thought, pushing those thoughts aside. *Time enough for blame later. We must be focused!*

Light-orbs lit the way, though dimly. The women's shadows flickered and bounced across the walls like dancing skeletons. Kailene knew these hallways well, having traversed them many times as part of her security inspections. Much good it has done us, she thought grimly. So much for all my preparations! To her right down the hall was the kitchen sub-basement. It was the closest access to the floors above.

Upon entering the sub-basement level, she and Eleanor climbed the adjoining stairs to the main kitchen. Sword held upright in both hands, she pushed on the partly open doorway at the top of the steps with her shoulder.

A body lay crumpled behind it, its limbs akimbo as if the man had been trying to escape to the sub-basement. Blood soaked the back of his smock. "One of the kitchen staff," Kailene whispered. She and Eleanor moved quickly and quietly into the kitchen, defensive postures assumed, bodies at a crouch, swords at the ready. The stone ovens glowed with heat; the smell of baking bread filled the huge brick-lined room; butchered hens lay on chopping blocks; gutted hogs, quant and deer carcasses hung on racks from the ceiling; fruit and various utensils lay scattered over the stone-tiled floor.

But another smell, that of death, lingered here as well. The blood running in the floor gutters to the drainage grates did not all belong to animals. "There are more bodies over here," Eleanor hissed from behind one of the utility sinks. "Marcel is among them."

The First Chef, Kailene winced. A good man she recalled from her brief contacts with him. How had the Perliox gained entrance so quickly? *No,* Kailene thought as she turned toward a sound emanating from the adjoining pantry. *Not the Perliox.*

Laughter and the shattering of dishes... Kailene hand-signaled Eleanor as each took up a position at the sides of the pantry entranceway. At Kailene's nod, both Knight-Wardens rushed in, swords held high.

Three of the Set's paladins turned from the giant wall-length cupboards, which they had been ransacking. Surprise showed on their helmless faces. They lounged easily and carelessly, wearing no armor as if they feared no danger and the Set belonged to them. Two held open steins filled with ale. Their still-drawn swords were covered in blood.

"Percin," Kailene said, reflecting her own shock and outrage. "What have you done?"

The First Paladin smiled, raising his sword. "Ah, Marshal," he said, his eyes glinting. "Joyous Frenten's Eve to you." He cocked his head, a puzzled expression flickering over his face as if he had just remembered something important. "You were not supposed to survive the explosion."

"What?" Kailene shivered with dread. "What are you talking about?"

In answer, the three troopers charged.

და

BORTRUM

With Bortrum supporting and moving himself forward on his crutches and Aermisiny leading the way, the five comrades wound their way through the eerily empty corridors of the north wing of Set Olan.

It was as if a wind-djinn had swept the wing of life. They found the bodies of servants and a handful of clerics and nuns, cruelly murdered--some by the sword, some, it appeared, by the very poison given to them by Dantol or whatever was impersonating him.

"There is dark magic at work here." Aermisiny stopped at an open doorway and turned away, her face filled with revulsion. "Only such foul sorcery could kill so many so quickly." Bortrum's stomach turned at the sight inside. The storage area was piled high with bodies--gaping mouths and bulging eyes stared into nowhere out of ravaged, bloodless faces. The stench was horrific.

"The Priest-Mage," Solana said softly.

"Aye." Bortrum nodded. "He is in league with Dantol and the shifter."

"That would explain why any warding spells cast

around the Set didn't hold," Aermisiny said.

"It making no sense!" Solana cried. "Why Dantol allowing an attack on his own Set? His own people?"

"Perhaps he, too, is in thrall to this dark magic," Bortrum replied. "That would explain much."

"Unless he being dead."

Bortrum shook his head. "Yes, unless he's dead."

"Bortrum," Aermisiny said, a thoughtful though troubled look crossing her face. "Why hasn't Marcus tried to contact us? His farsensing can sometimes be reversed so that he can alert others to his whereabouts. I pray he's not been killed also."

"Or turned."

"Yes, that might be the worst of it."

"Shut the door, please." Bortrum closed his eyes. For the first time in a long time, he felt fear. Not for himself but for his wife and friends and the whole of Olan. What madness had overtaken the Set? And especially Dantol. He couldn't shake the feeling that he was involved in this.

"I hearing something." Solana had cocked her head to one side. "Fighting, I thinks. One voice being familiar..."

"Aye," Bortrum said, turning nimbly, despite his

handicap. "From the end of the hall..." He glanced at Solana as an odd expression flitted over the woman's features. She looked at both Bortrum and Aermisiny. "The Marshal. She being attacked."

Bortrum snapped to attention. "Go!" he commanded. Solana whirled and, using her Gift of Speed, ran down the corridor, a blur of motion. "Aermisiny, I can move quickly enough, still..." But his wife was already picking him up in her deceptively strong arms. *We could use the Marshal's help,* Bortrum thought. *If we are to stop this threat. I pray we are not too late.*

୫

KAILENE

Percin was big, probably twice Kailene's size and weight. She knew he had always resented her presence at the Set and now his anger and frustration erupted at her in full force. He swung his sword like a madman, driving her scrambling back out of the pantry and into the main kitchen.

"Filthy black whore!" Percin cried, his features contorted with animal rage.

Kailene stumbled, her sword arm trembling with the effort of blocking Percin's mighty blows. She recovered her balance just in time to avoid a lunging jab of Percin's weapon. She leaped over his next sweeping strike and, while still airborne, kicked out at his head.

Her foot clipped him on the temple, causing the First Paladin's head to snap back. He recovered instantly and swung a backhanded slash at the young marshal.

But Kailene had already done a backward flip out of Percin's reach to regain her footing. She grabbed a stone cooking pot and flung it at Percin. Out of the corner of her eye, she saw Eleanor battling only one of the two other paladins. But her second favored one arm, her shoulder wound bleeding.

Percin batted the pot away and attacked again, bringing his broadsword straight down at Kailene with both meaty hands. Kailene parried it with her own sword but was driven back against a chopping block by the force of the blow. Pain surged up her back from the edge of the block. Her arms throbbed as she pushed her blade against Percin's.

The First Paladin pressed downward, his greater strength forcing both blades toward Kailene's neck. Spittle flew from his mouth; his eyes were glazed; his breath reeked of ale. Desperately, Kailene tried to kick the paladin but the big man's body was too close. Kailene grunted, trying to hold on. She felt like her back was breaking. Rowt! she called from her Eye, playing a hunch. A fuzzy image--the woods behind the fortress-temple, the jerking motion of frantic running. Her hound was on his way to the Set but would never make it in time.

Suddenly, something ran behind Percin, something so fast the pots and utensils still hanging from the ceiling racks swung at its passing. Percin cried out and arched his body away from Kailene, his head thrown up as a spray of blood spurted from behind him. Crying out in relief, Kailene rolled away from between Percin and the chopping block, turned and plunged her blade into the First Paladin's side.

With a strangled cry, Percin fell to the floor. Kailene whirled toward the pantry as Eleanor stumbled from the small room, barely able to walk. "Eleanor!" Kailene took hold of her second with a free arm, trying to support her. Behind her, in the pantry, lay the bodies of the other two paladins.

"Good work. Easy, easy..."

"They were drunk," Eleanor rasped, trying to smile. "I... I had no problem." But Eleanor had sustained more wounds in her struggle with the two guards. Despite Kailene's help, she fell to her knees.

Drunk yes, Kailene thought with a frown as she remembered the crazed look on Percin's face. *But more than that--Percin and the others were in thrall to some outside force.*

"She needing curing."

Kailene jerked her head up. The woman named Solana stood in front of her, a bloody knife in her hand. "You," she whispered to the tall woman. "That... that was you?"

Solana nodded, looking back toward Percin's body. "I running pretty fast, heya? You should seeing me when I being younger!"

A merchant... warrior? "My... my thanks, noble lady."

At that moment, the man called Bortrum was carried into the kitchen by the small woman... Aermisiny? <u>Surely one so small isn't strong enough to carry someone that quickly?</u> Kailene wondered. And yet, there she was.

Bortrum took one look at Eleanor and Kailene and said, pointing at Eleanor, "Let me have her first. She's the more serious."

"What?" Kailene asked, feeling suddenly weak. Blood was once more running from her head wound. The room started spinning. "What do you mean?"

"I possess the Gift of Healing. Give her to me." The Gift of Healing? Kailene blinked. The histories told of such a Gift.

Solana helped steady a barely conscious Eleanor as Aermisiny brought Bortrum closer and set him on his feet where he balanced himself with his crutches. The cripple put his hand on Eleanor's chest, pressed his forehead to hers and closed his eyes.

Kailene wasn't sure what happened next--was she seeing things? The air seemed to shimmer around her

83

second and the Ofrikane; there was a gentle radiance...
After a few moments, Bortrum slumped over, sweating
and breathing hard. Eleanor wobbled a little and then
looked up, blinking as if she had just awakened. The
bleeding from her wounds had stopped.

"How...?" But Aermisiny was already
maneuvering Bortrum close to Kailene. Solana knelt
behind Kailene and took hold of her shoulders. Despite
her pain and the situation, Kailene felt a thrill, realizing
that she relished the older woman's touch. If only...

Bortrum reached out to her...

℮

84

THOMAS

Thomas watched in shock as the sky-ships hovered like fat obscene raptors--one over the Set and the other over the city itself. As if giving birth, both disgorged long tether lines from their underbellies, which the warriors aboard used to shimmy down to the ground.

Their armor, the way they move... Thomas jerked with shocked recognition. *They are Perliox!* He looked below wildly. *There is no time to get help,* he thought. *I must act! I pray Solana and the rest can fend for themselves!*

He launched himself from the tower, flying straight for the nearest ship. Multiple tethers hung from the belly hatches like sinewy tentacles. Dozens of Perliox troopers slid downward, their red eyes glowing through the slits in their plumed helmets. Metal spikes sprouted from their shoulder and hip guards; silver breastplates marked with the sigil of the Perliox Ascendancy glittered in the light; broadswords and maces hung at the troopers' belts.

I thought I would never see such a sight again. Thomas neared the ship, heading for the top observatory deck. *There is a way. They won't expect someone to attack them from the air.*

He rose above the ship, setting his sights on its outdoor maintenance deck constructed at the very roof of the craft. There stood three Perliox, judging from their lack of armor, not soldiers but flight crew, no doubt seeing to some navigational aspect of the ship. The sky-ships were large and formidable; their cloth bulk was held inside a skeleton of wood and metal. But a delicate balance had to be maintained between their weight and the flammable gas that powered them, Thomas knew from his studies of flight scrolls. Anything that took to the air was an interest of his. If he could upset that balance... One of the Perliox pointed at Thomas, screaming a warning to his fellows.

Ah, Thomas, thought. This will make things more difficult. He dove, angling his flight to the right of the ship and then swooping up and around to get behind the three. Two of the Perliox whirled. Flight crew or not, they raised crossbows and fired. The deadly metal shafts streaked by Thomas on either side of him as he pulled his wings in close to his body and dropped straight down.

Arms outstretched and fists clenched, he

slammed into two of the Perliox. Too late, he saw the flash of steel in the light. He pulled up, gasping at the sudden pain in his right side. Blood collected below his armpit, whipping into the wind. He had been cut--a blade had found its mark.

But he had done it! One of the Perliox had disappeared over the side, falling to his death. One other lay on the deck, seemingly unconscious. The third, holding the knife that had wounded Thomas, looked upward at the attacking Gifted One and then wildly about him, confused.

I won't give him a chance to get below deck. Gritting his teeth against the pain and sudden lightheadedness he felt, he dropped downward once again.

₧₦

BORTRUM

Weak and dizzy, Bortrum fell backwards into his wife's arms. He had expended much of his Gift's energy in too short a time. And he was old. He needed to rest longer and more often now. He felt Aermisiny's small hands on him, soothing, reassuring, renewing his strength.

The Marshal and her guard were looking at each other in amazement, their wounds healed. They felt their bodies, shaking their heads in disbelief. Yet, Bortrum could tell that an abrupt realization had dawned on Kailene. *Aye, she's a clever one,* he thought. *She has figured it out.* The young Ofrikane whispered something to her guard, whose eyes widened in astonishment. Both knelt and bowed their heads.

"Sacred Ones," Kailene said in a whispered, respectful voice. "Forgive us. We didn't know..."

Bortrum snorted. "Nonsense, sister!" he said. "Please, both of you. Do not kneel to us. We're no more sacred than you are."

Kailene stood slowly, looking from Solana to Aermisiny to Bortrum. "A Gift of Healing," she said,

pointing to Bortrum and then to Solana, "And of Speed."
It seemed her gaze lingered on the tall woman. She then
turned and studied Aermisiny. "You have the one of
Strength, I'll wager. And there is the fat one--he of the
Farsensing ability."

She looked toward Bortrum as if for
acknowledgement. "The one called Thomas--he is no
hunchback."

"His 'hump' are his wings--he possesses the Gift
of Flight," Bortrum finished for her. "And, aye, there are
two of us who have passed on--Wing-Ma, he with the
Gift of Seeing, blind though he was, and Feersah,
controlling the Gift of Fire." He paused, looking away
before continuing, "though much good it did both of
them at the end."

"The Sacred Seven," Kailene's guard murmured.

Aermisiny sighed. "What's left of us."

"You helped win the Battle of Set Perl!"
Kailene's eyes shone with reverence and awe. "I've read
the history scrolls so many times. Glimmerlaan
prefecture and the whole of the Imperium owe you a
great debt! Never did I think that I would stand here
with you. You are like gods to us!"

"Please, sister, we have no time for misplaced

hero worship. Our exploits have been made into much more than they really are." *And, as a result, our true accomplishments have become insignificant and forgotten.* Bortrum positioned himself straighter, feeling uncomfortable at the young woman's words. *Aye,* he thought. *The Gifted Ones are still feared or held in contempt in most prefectures. What good did we really do? Has anything really changed?*

"Believe me, we're not gods, only people like you with an added talent that we have been able to use for good. And now we must work together. Foul deeds have been done today, right under our very noses." Quickly Bortrum told Kailene of Dantol's possibly traitorous act and the appearance of the mysterious shifter. "It seems at least some of the Set's paladin guard are working with Dantol as well, not to mention the Priest-Mage. Only the Almighty One knows how many more."

"Aye, there was the First Prelate," Kailene said, a thoughtful look on her night-colored face. "He seemed pensive, almost as if he was expecting something. And yet he sounded the alarm."

Bortrum pursed his lips. "That too may have been part of the plan, to bring the others out into the courtyard, to inflict the most damage."

"That makes a clever sense." In turn, the Marshal outlined the events that had happened at the gates and in the kitchen and told of her suspicion of outside influence.

"Sky-ships?" Aermisiny wondered. "And explosive devices. Clearly, Dantol supplied that exotic weaponry from these new factories of his as he did in the past--how else could the Perliox get such? They have been in exile for forty turnings. The Bishop-Prefect has accomplished much since he became ruler here, it seems. He employs those weapons that helped defeat the Perliox once to now attack his own people!"

"And we helped put him in that position," Bortrum added.

"But, I asking again," Solana said. She looked nervous and fidgety. Bortrum knew, in her anxiety, that she wanted to run, to utilize her Gift. "Why? Why he forging an alliance with the Perliox? Why he attacking us?"

"And why were the five of you brought here at the same time as the conference?" Kailene added. "I questioned that decision but was overruled."

"No time to talk now," Bortrum said. "We must

find Dantol. We must go straight to the heart of this!"

"We'll need help too," Kailene added. "Reinforcements but I'd wager all communication lines have been cut--flyers, homing-fowl, runners. We'll have been isolated if they were to make this plan of theirs work completely."

"But that being another question, heya? What being this plan?"

Kailene shot Bortrum a frustrated look. *This young one is ready for action,* he reasoned. *She feels responsible.* "I can send my hounds with a message to Fort Pennit," the Marshal said. "But I don't know what kind of shape they're in." A pause. "One may be dead."

"I being one runner not isolated!" Solana's previous fear was now gone, Bortrum noted, replaced by another, more resolved emotion. Here was something she could do. "I being the one to go."

Still, they needed to plan this. "Solana..."

"There being a back way out?" Solana asked of Kailene.

"Solana!"

Solana turned to Bortrum, her eyes suddenly glimmering with tears. "Like Thomas be saying--we being here before, heya? I logical one to go to Fort

Pennit. I being old but still run faster than the Perliox and the Marshall's hounds. Thomas be fighting sky-ships, knowing him. He's a loner, always being one, and no good to us now."

"She's right," Aermisiny said. "Thomas should have been back by now."

"There is a hidden rear door that goes below ground and out beyond the Set's walls." Kailene began. "The old royal bolt-hole designed by the Perliox when they ruled here."

"Show me!" Solana looked at Bortrum and Aermisiny. "I be coming back." Aermisiny ran to Solana and embraced the tall woman.

"The Almighty One protect you." Bortrum felt a sense of doom envelop him as Kailene led Solana off down the corridor. *I pray you will come back,* he thought. *And I pray we'll be here when you do.*

∞

KAILENE

Kailene took Solana through a series of dark, angled corridors, the bolt-hole's location etched in her mind as her position as Marshal demanded. They met no one in the empty hallways, living or dead. The subbasement corridors were silent as tombs. As the two of them made their way, Kailene began to think they were the only ones left alive anywhere in the Set.

And perhaps I wouldn't even be here if not for Bortrum. She marveled again at the healing powers of the crippled merchant. The histories, the legends, all the stories were true. *No,* she chastised herself. *He is anything but crippled and he is not a merchant--he is a Sacred One!*

Which posed a problem for her. Kailene was attracted to this woman following her, an attraction she thought had been reciprocated. But then to know Solana was one of the Sacred Seven! Kailene felt the fool for her presumptuousness.

"Here it is," Kailene said finally, forcing her thoughts back to the problem at hand. She pulled her set of master keys from her belt pouch, not looking up at her companion. She knelt to unlock the circular door inset into the floor.

Both women had to use their combined strength to lift the door open from its rounded moorings. It looked like it hadn't been opened in a long time. A ladder led downwards.

Solana had already procured a torch from one of the wall niches and had set one foot on the ladder's first rung. She paused, holding Kailene's gaze. "I asking a boon, heya?" she said, her lower lip trembling. "I not knowing you but I feeling your heat."

Kailene blinked, taken aback by so bold a statement. And yet, it was true.

"You be seeing Thomas, the winged one, tell him... tell him I wishing it could be different." The older woman's face filled with pain, her voice turned hoarse with emotion.

Kailene shook her head. What was this all about? Did she love this Thomas? Why didn't she tell him herself? Because she preferred women? "Please, noble lady, have your friends tell him," the Marshal said, biting back her sudden discomfort. "Why ask me?"

"You not one of us." Solana looked down. "I cannot be saying why for certain I trusting you," she whispered. "I don't wanting Bortrum or Aermisiny to be knowing. Thomas and I... once, long ago we..." The woman's eyes filled with sudden tears. "We having a child--Thomas not knowing. No one knowing. Just you now and the priests of Set Xalatar. Our son raised there at the Set--being a scholar, I hoping, he having his own Gift. You be letting Thomas know, heya? He deserving to know after all this time."

A noise sounded from further down the corridor-- voices. "Someone's coming!" Kailene hissed. "Please go!"

"Eeeyah, promise me!" Solana's own heat was turned up now, her body radiating it in waves. "If I not coming back..."

"Aye, aye! I'll tell him. Go!"

Solana cupped Kailene's cheek in her hand, a look of resigned finality drawn on her features. This close, Kailene could see the lines in the Gifted One's face, the many years reflected in those abruptly sad eyes. Kailene moved closer, wanting to comfort her, wanting to... Solana stepped back, made a sound, a wrenching sob, and then descended into the bolt-hole.

Kailene closed and relocked the door, momentarily shaken at the emotion and loss radiating from the Gifted One. Then, with a deep breath, she drew her sword and started moving back toward the kitchen. The noises she had heard were closer now. *Troopers,* she thought, analyzing the fragments of sound drifting toward her. *Paladins maybe. And coming this way.*

Rowt, she thought, entering her Eye. Her hound had followed her mental spoor. He was fast and he was close. Images of the sub-level door where Kailene and Eleanor had entered coalesced--broken through by the Perliox. Rowt, too had followed the enemy, gaining entrance the same way.

And he was alone. Kailene forced back the grief building within her. Ayo must be dead--her Eye picked up no traces of the hound.

Rowt, to me. Unsheathing her sword, she moved back the way she had come.

ઇ

SOLANA

Solana traversed the tunnel quickly but not as quickly as she desired. She itched to be running, to prove she could still be of value (besides her wretched jewelry making!) but any faster and the torch would go out. The tunnel smelled of disuse, mold and age. She cringed in disgust as cockroaches and other nocturnal vermin scuttled at the torch's light. Apparently, no one at the Set had needed to use the bolt-hole in a long while. She wondered if anyone even remembered it was here besides the Marshal. Only Kailene knew because of the Ofrikane's duties, Solana was sure.

The north wing was situated near the rear of the Set so Solana knew she must reach the end of the tunnel soon. There! The murky shape of a ladder loomed ahead.

As she climbed the rungs upward, Solana realized too late that the door above her might need a key to unlock it as well. And where would she come out if she did manage to get it open? Straight into the arms of the hated Perliox? How did that cruel race escape their guarding spells? *I wishing Aermisiny here now,* she thought as she grasped the latch and, straining, pushed. *I needing her strength.*

The door creaked open, heavy with rust and the passing of time, the lock breaking easily. Solana grunted and shoved, her aged muscles burning with the effort. Dirt and gravel spilled into the entranceway; dust swirled around her. Streaks of light illuminated what looked to be a small cave. She took a deep breath and coughed in the sour, close air.

Dropping the torch back into the tunnel, Solana scrabbled out of the bolt-hole and poked her way through the weed and creeper-choked cave entrance. She was somewhere within a small grove of trees behind Set Olan, out of the city itself to the rear of the tournament fields.

Solana gasped in surprise. The tournament fields--this was where the last battle had taken place those long turnings ago. It was here that Bortrum had lost the use of his legs; here that Feersah had met her demise before Set Perl had become Set Olan. *We being so young,* Solana thought in sadness. *So young...*

She pushed back the unwanted memories and looked again. From beneath a large oak and across the closely cropped acreage that served the jousting and equestrian events (set up now up for Frenten's Eve celebrations), she could see the smoke and flame rising from the besieged Set. She could see the sky-ships floating above the fortress-temple like carrion-eaters; she could see a large contingent of the Perliox moving towards the rear of the city's walls; she could see...

Thomas, she realized, recognizing the winged figure. He looked like a gnat buzzing around a falcon. *I knew it!* "Be having a care, my old love," she whispered. She removed her shoes and tore her gown up to her hips, ripping that portion off to give her legs room to move. She took several deep breaths, quickly stretched, turned and started running.

ℭ

THOMAS

Thomas struck the remaining crewman feet-first in the back as the Perliox attempted to get to the side access ladder. The Perliox fell to the deck, his knife clattering from his hand. Grimacing in pain from his own wound, Thomas scooped the weapon up and glided to the opposite end of the ship. He lighted on another small deck, this one equipped with a network of small tubes and vented apertures. *It's here,* he thought, searching. *The upper gas flue.*

Yes! Thomas recognized the design of the flue from the scrolls he had studied. The flues of the sky-ships held a fatal flaw, so it was recorded. If he could cause a spark...

But if he succeeded, the ship would crash into Set Olan. *No,* he reasoned. *The gas will ignite and eviscerate the entire craft before it hits the ground or any structures. It will be that fast. I have to do it!*

Gritting his teeth, he jammed the knife into the metal grate covering the flue. Back and forth, metal against metal, he ran the knife through the flue. Until...

A spark! Thomas watched the flash of light

ignite, rushing backwards through the flue like a maddened firefly. Dropping the knife he pushed upward and launched himself to the side of the sky-ship. Just as he spread his wings, a searing pain ripped through his leg.

Thomas screamed as he grabbed his leg, flipping over and over. A crossbow bolt protruded through his right calf, puncturing cleanly through his muscles. Had it struck a bone, the bolt would have exploded upon impact as he had seen happening below. Thomas struggled to remain airborne, his wings flapping desperately. He saw one of the Perliox crewmen had regained consciousness, reloaded and fired his weapon. Even now, he loaded yet another bolt.

Must gain some height... Thomas righted himself and ascended, his wings burning with the pain of effort, his side and leg spouting blood. *Must make sure Solana is safe.*

It was as if a star had fallen to earth. The sky-ship exploded in a huge ball of fire, streamers of flame blossoming outward like the rays of the sun. Thomas cried out as a whirlwind of heat and flame engulfed him.

ෂ

KAILENE

"There she is! The farsenser was right!"

There were six of them--Perliox troopers. Their armor and swords were wet with the blood of their victims; their very presence reflected the death lust coursing through them. *Must keep them away from the Sacred Ones,* Kailene thought, giving no thought to what the leader had just said. *Give Bortrum and Aermisiny time to get to the Bishop-Prefect.* She shouted a challenge to the enemy, holding her sword out in front of her, gripping it tightly so the troopers wouldn't see her hands shaking. She remembered her teachings then, the strength and support from all of those she loved. *Father,* she thought, gritting her teeth. *I honor your memory with this battle!*

She charged *them,* swinging her sword in the series of windmilling moves she had learned as a Knight-Warden-in-Training--moves of the ancient pen-rae defense mode designed to fend off more than one attacker. She had always been the best student at pen-rae, some innate force within her allowing her to utilize it well, at times, even more proficiently than her teacher.

She prayed it would help her now.

Kailene got past the first two troopers, felling one with an arcing blow to the neck. She moved swiftly and fluidly, ducking under one sweeping blade thrust as she cocked her left wrist to release the forearm dagger from its holster into her hand.

She whirled around to prick a Perliox in his exposed chin with the dagger. The fast-acting poison the dagger excreted took hold almost instantly, dropping the trooper to the floor.

Her Inner Eye, even without her hounds' help, focused her senses and concentrated the pen-rae, honing in on the outpouring of energy of those she fought. It was as if she could see and hear everything in slow motion. She felt the air as it rolled away from the Perliox, identifying their positions even if she couldn't see them; their breath, the hissing of their swords as they were swung--she could perceive them--each sound, each noise identified and located. But not for long. Her Eye could only do so much in so concentrated a time. Kailene had to act quickly before its power and her own burst of energy faded.

She rolled away from two stabbing blows, hitting the floor in a crouch, only to block a third while on her knees. Falling backwards, she whipped her leg out to catch the nearest trooper in the ankles, upending him onto his back.

Somersaulting backwards onto her feet, she parried another deadly thrust but the three remaining troopers moved toward her, backing her up against the wall. She struck at them with her sword and the forearm blade, just managing to keep them at bay. "Cowards!" Kailene cried. "You will not get this Set without a fight!"

A large, dark shape shot out of the shadows. Silent and deadly, it grabbed the trooper nearest Kailene by his sword arm with great and powerful jaws and pulled him to the floor. The trooper screamed as his arm was twisted and torn viciously from its roots. "Rowt!" Kailene shouted. "I want one alive!"

Taking advantage of the distraction caused by her hound, Kailene lunged forward and speared one of the Perliox through a seam in his stomach armor. By the time she had pulled her sword free of the dying trooper, Rowt had pinned the last of the enemy to the floor.

"Good boy, my strong Rowt," Kailene said breathlessly as she knelt by the downed trooper. She fought back the laughter bubbling up in her throat--by the Seven, they had done it! Rowt leaned his great weight on the trapped Perliox, his fangs bared and slavering, his body trembling in animal fury. Almost as big as a pony, the mountain canine was sleekly built and black as night. He growled in the face of the Perliox, barely controlling his feral wrath. An image exploded in Kailene's Eye, communicated by Rowt and confirming her own suspicions--Ayo, her pet and comrade and Rowt's litter-mate--dead.

On my family's honor, on the soul of the mother I never knew--I will make them pay.

"Information," Kailene hissed, her momentary elation crumbling. Blinking back sudden tears, she pushed her bloody sword blade against the trooper's neck. "I want it now, vile scum." Anger surged through Kailene as well, making it almost impossible to contain herself. These demon Perliox had killed her friends, her beloved Ayo and those she had sworn to protect, just like they had done so many turnings ago to the people of Glimmerlaan prefecture. Filth! The armies of the Imperium should have destroyed them all when they had the chance.

"Kai!" Eleanor rushed down the corridor, the two Sacred Ones, Bortrum and Aermisiny, right behind her.

Kailene's second stopped, surveying the carnage wrought by her marshal and the hound. "Well done!" she cried proudly. "Our old teacher, Phillino, would be pleased."

"Eleanor..."

Eleanor straightened to attention, heeding the edge to Kailene's voice. "We heard the fighting and came as quickly as we could. Plus there was an explosion, outside. We think one of the sky-ships has been destroyed! Nothing else could make such a sound."

Kailene answered with a brusque nod. "Where is your leader?" she demanded of her prisoner. "And the Bishop-Prefect? Your insignia is of a high-ranking officer, one who would know such information. Tell me or my hound will rip you to pieces!"

Eleanor stepped up, adding her sword to Kailene's. She smiled a malicious grin. "Speak, pig! And maybe we'll let you live. I could use a Perliox for target practice."

"Yes, yes! I will tell you!" The Perliox's voice was low and guttural and shook with fear. Even warriors such as these could be broken so easily. The mountain hounds, those that had been blessed with farsensing, could radiate fear and control to a degree. This enemy felt that in waves. "The Holy Sanctum, behind the Nave of the Pantocrator. They have gone there." Yet still he fought back. "But that won't save you. You almost destroyed our people once, you and your official pogroms, your heinous 'tribal cleansing.' It won't happen again. We will take back our land. We will..."

He stopped, his fiery eyes widening. "You," he said softly, looking at Kailene. "You are one of us. This close, I see it now. The way you fought. Your blood must be..."

Rowt! Kailene stood and walked away as her hound tore into the screaming trooper. What had that filth been talking about? *Lies,* she thought at the Perliox's last words. *Propaganda and trickery. The Perliox were lucky just to be exiled. The history scrolls have recorded their atrocities!*

"Kai?" Eleanor voice was low, disbelieving, despite her usual braggadocio. "He was unarmed. We could have just bound him..."

"Yes! Was that necessary?" Bortrum interrupted with a frown, moving in front of Kailene. The Ofrikane merchant and his diminutive lady stood disapprovingly. "Aye, the Perliox are monsters but that one may have provided more useful information."

"We have enough," Kailene spat, trying to push thoughts of Ayo out of her mind, of the strange things the Perliox had said at the very end. Her blood? One of us? What did that mean?

"And there was this..." She looked at Bortrum and Aermisiny. "Right before they attacked, one of them said, 'The farsenser was right.'"

She watched the Healer's reaction. Both he and the woman looked as if they had been struck. "That would mean he senses us coming," Bortrum began slowly. "That he sent the troopers to kill us."

"Indeed." Kailene holstered the forearm dagger, her hand shaking, wondering what Phillino would think of her actions now. "We go to the Holy Sanctum and hope your Solana has reached Fort Pennit. If the Bishop-Prefect and the Perliox leader and perhaps your friend, Marcus, are where this one said they would be, we must stop them!"

❧

SOLANA

Solana heard the explosion behind her as she ran. It was if the very heavens had been ripped apart. Her heart clenched in her chest, knowing that Thomas had probably caused the blast, knowing, too, that it had probably killed him.

This being my last run, I'm wagering, she thought, refusing to look back. *Very well then. I making it for you, Thomas! And our son!* She sprinted along the edge of the forest bordering the gaming fields. There, up ahead, near the rocky foothills of the northern Olan range, was a cleft in the rocks that could short-cut her to Fort Pennit. If it was unguarded, if nothing had changed in the last forty turnings...

A cry from behind her--she had been spotted by the enemy divisions attacking Set Olan from the rear. A crossbow bolt whizzed by on either side of her, erupting in flashes of smoke and fire as they struck the ground. Dodging flying debris, she finally risked a glance over her shoulder. Several Perliox on horseback were racing toward her, breaking away from the main group. More bolts were being loaded even as the troopers' mounts strained at their bits, froth flying from their mouths.

Solana's legs and arms pumped furiously. Her feet whispered over the ground as she accelerated. More explosions sounded behind her--if one of the bolts got even a little too close...

More shouts, the thunder of the horses' hooves. The cleft in the rock loomed ahead. Solana turned up the speed, her heart and lungs churning, her muscles straining like they never had before. Something was whistling through the air right behind her, gaining. One of the bolts...

She angled into the cleft as the bolt hit the hill straight on behind her and exploded. Solana ran upward over the rocks, her callused, bare feet finding toeholds to propel her forward. Free! she exulted as she cut again to the left and headed downwards toward the river. Now faster still. She must get to Fort Pennit for help before it was too late.

ॐ

BORTRUM

Bortrum and the others stood in the Nave of the Pantocrator. Surrounded by towering stained-glass windows and arching columns, the nave was the largest of the many chapels that Set Olan housed.

How much it has changed in the last forty turnings, Bortrum thought, marveling at the new construction and adornment. Soft red carpet covered the floor in plush elegance as it flowed upward to the altar where once furs and stone had roughly lain. Gold candelabras and chandeliers glittered like jewels in the place where sacrifices had been made. Side entries led to tombs and reliquaries housing artifacts both old and new. Paintings and sculptures covered almost every space of the now ornate chamber's walls and ceiling while huge, elaborate proskinitarions displayed icons of the Olanides' gods, saints and heroes in place of the barbarous idols once revered here by the Perliox. Here, the Bishop-Prefect led the worship services himself and held court for the most notable personages of the prefecture.

The old deities are gone from here now, Bortrum

reflected. *All traces of those who had been our enemy are gone.*

The comrades' journey from the north wing to the central narthex of the church proper had been uneventful except for the countless signs of death--more corpses littered the way, this time many seeming to have fallen from some kind of affliction in addition to the violence.

"Spell-sickness," Aermisiny had explained after reluctantly examining the dead. "Any poor unfortunate ensorcelled so powerfully for too long a time becomes like these--bruised skin, bleeding eyes, swollen glands, ruptured organs. More evidence pointing to the Priest-Mage."

"Has he magicked the whole Set?" Bortrum wondered aloud. Leaning on his crutches, he scratched his aching stump irritably. "He is old and was never *that* powerful, existing mainly as a figurehead. How could he have done all this?" He looked aloft now at the interior of the nave's great dome. The Pantocrator--the Almighty One, ruler of all the gods of the Imperium--looked down on him and his comrades from a giant painted, bejeweled and gold-leafed face. *Give me answers, Almighty One,* Bortrum prayed. *I need your guidance.*

There was a snuffling sound--the hound barked

urgently. "Noble lord and lady," Kailene announced from the altar. "Over here. Rowt has found something."

Aermisiny picked Bortrum up and, cradling him once again like a child, mounted the chancel steps to the altar. The young Marshal and her surviving hound stood near a body, almost hidden in the flickering, candlelit shadows. Bortrum felt an icy cold grip his heart. "The Priest-Mage," he muttered. "Dead with the spell-sickness himself. How...?"

"It's the Perliox," Kailene said, her features hardened. "They must have one of their Animists with them. It's the only way they could have overcome the Set. He must have taken control of the Priest-Mage and, through him, the others."

This young one has studied the enemy's ways. Bortrum paused, abruptly saddened, remembering his own encountering with one of the Perliox magickers long ago. *And here, on her first watch, becomes hardened from the reality of them.* "And combined his magic with the Priest-Mage's--against his will to attack his his own people," he finished. "Insidious." *And yet effective. I can still see Feersah falling...*

The hound suddenly backed up a step, his hackles rising. A growl escaped his throat. Both he and his young mistress whirled toward the back of the chancel.

The doors to the Holy Sanctum flew open. Two figures emerged from the chamber beyond, both startlingly familiar.

"Marcus!" Bortrum gasped. The rotund farsenser stood with Dantol, the Bishop-Prefect. *A friend no more,* Bortrum lamented. "Are you well, Marcus?"

"Let the Sacred One go, Your Grace." Kailene and her second took up a position between Bortrum and Aermisiny and the Bishop-Prefect. The hound growled a warning. "Stand aside."

At that moment, Rowt began to tremble, his tail suddenly tucked between his legs. The hound whined, turned in a circle and pressed up against his mistress.

Kailene's head jerked as she stumbled back a step, her free hand reaching out for her dog. Her second came to her aid, keeping one eye on Dantol.

What is he doing? "Marcus!" Bortrum cried. "Stop it! Stop invading their minds."

"No!" Marcus shouted, his eyes shining with some fiery emotion. His enormous body shook as if he was on the verge of convulsing. "I take no more orders from you, Bortrum. It's time to rewrite the scrolls of history. It's time to tell the truth about what happened at the Battle of Olan so many turnings ago when Set Olan was called Set Perl. About how we attacked the Perliox Ascendancy here at their ancestral home out of fear and racist hate. How we stripped a peaceful people of their humanity and turned them into monsters."

೮೦

THOMAS

Thomas screamed in pain. Gasping for breath, he forced himself to pull the scrap of cloth he had torn from his shirt tighter around his upper chest. The cloth managed to close the wound in his side but he knew it wouldn't stop the bleeding for very long. He huddled in the shelter of a stone gable, sharing the space with a gargoyle-carved downspout. The life-sized statue stood broken, damaged by age and disrepair.

We are alike, you and I, he thought, silently addressing the rock-hewn creature. *Both monsters nearing our end.*

Below him, the flaming remnants of the destroyed sky-ship fluttered to earth. I did it, he thought, not without some amazed pride. *But how did I survive?* He paused, watching the second sky-ship begin to ascend. Its pilots had seen the destruction of its comrade. Did they now try to escape whatever "secret weapon," whatever "sky-ship killer," the Set possessed? He almost laughed out loud, wondering again, *Why did I survive? An old man like me?*

His wings were singed; his calf throbbed with the

crossbow bolt still lodged in its muscle. He dared not try to remove it now in case its explosive workings detonated. He hung his head in pain and despair. *This cowardly attack,* he thought. *Monstrous. Monstrous.*

And yet, it could have been worse, he knew. There seemed to be no more Perliox troopers swarming into the city. Why? Olan was at their mercy.

Perhaps there was still hope.

He tried to work it through his pain-befuddled mind, tried to determine what his comrades would be doing. *If they are still alive, they might attempt to get help.* His head snapped up. *Solana would volunteer to go for reinforcements, she is so stubborn and hard-headed--Fort Pennit. It is the closest outpost and she can run there the fastest.*

He stood shakily, his body wracked with pain. *I must find her,* he thought with a grimace. *She may need help herself.* And then the thoughts he feared most flickered within his mind--*I must give the warning myself--if she doesn't make it. If she dies.*

Shrugging off that unbearable thought, Thomas spread his wings, ignored the pain as best he could and stepped into the wind.

ಐ

SOLANA

Solana's heart thudded against her ribs. She gasped for breath. Fort Pennit was in sight, but her old body was starting to fail her. She hadn't run so fast and so far in a long time. *Just being a little further... just a little...*

The Fort was several leagues south of Set Olan but she had traversed that distance in a very, very short time. Desperation and reckless need were the necessary fuel to her running, urging her on faster and faster.

Once upon a time, so long ago, she remembered Bortrum had tried to organize the Gifted Ones, to bring them all together in a sort of protective guild. Then, they could have acted together to help one another, to give each other the solace and comfort they might need in a world so cruel and unjust. But those times were past.

Fool, she thought. *Old selfish fool. Oh!*

The pain in her chest was like a knife ripping her vitals. She screamed, stumbling as her left arm went numb. Her pace slowed even as she continued pounding down the brick-inlaid main road to the fort's entrance gates, decorated for Frenten's Eve with wreaths and bells. She could hear the watchman announcing her coming, could see the archers manning the battlements, could hear orders shouted.

Her good arm went up over her head, her hand forming the finger-signal for parlay. The gates began to open...

She fell as the pain tore through her. She hit the road hard, her breath coming in strangled gasps. Her body arched in agony. Overhead, just before she blacked out, she thought she saw a large bird soaring toward the fort. No, not a bird, she realized in wonder as the winged figure spiraled lower. An angel...

ℯ

Later, as she lay somewhere soft and comforting, the angel came to her. Solana knew then she would soon pass through the Veil. The angel was a herald of the Almighty One--a harbinger of death. If only she had warned the fort! If only she had been in time! She had failed, like she had failed Thomas and their son so long ago.

"Forgive me," she rasped between dry, cracked lips.

"There is nothing to forgive," the angel answered softly and gently. "I know about our son. I've always known." Ragged, limping and covered in blood, the angel whispered that he had given the alarm, that even now troopers were on their way to aid Olan, using their fastest horses and newly motorized conveyances to get there as swiftly as Solana had done.

He knelt over her, embracing her, covering her spent body with his burnt and ragged wings like a giant leathery blanket. "Solana," he said softly, in a voice she suddenly knew. "Solana."

⬧

KAILENE

Kailene fought the searing presence in her head. It was as if a fire burned at her brain. Her Eye had been penetrated and used as a conduit for this sudden violation. *The farsenser!* she thought, falling to her knees. *He* is *working against us!*

"Hold your ground," the one called Marcus commanded. He seemed a different person--more confident, in control. "And put down your weapons. I can cripple this sweet young Marshal's mind. You know I can do it, Bortrum. I did it at the Battle of Olan, to my everlasting shame, and I will do it now if I must."

"You bloated ox..." Eleanor brought her sword up. Kailene saw Marcus take a step toward her second, an intense look on his face. Rowt whined anew.

"No!" Kailene croaked. "Eleanor, stand down." Despite her pain, the Marshal had seen movement beyond in the Holy Sanctum. No telling how many others were there, waiting to attack. If they could keep the fat one talking, perhaps there might be a way to reverse this situation. Grudgingly, Eleanor backed off and, after a quick, heated glance in Kailene's direction, set her sword on the floor.

Kailene released her own weapon as the pain in her head subsided. She held onto Rowt--the hound had regained his focus and his courage and was straining towards Marcus and the religious ruler.

"Marcus?" the Sacred One called Bortrum asked, his voice steady but edged with an undercurrent of disbelief. Aermisiny still held him but it was evident to Kailene that another sort of control and power emanated from the crippled one. This one was outraged indeed. "What have you done?"

"He is ensorcelled like the others," Aermisiny said.

"No!" Marcus cried, his face turning red. "I do this of my own free will."

Kailene rose to her full height. "Murder and betrayal? That is the choice your free will has picked for you?" A quick glance behind her showed a handful of the Set's paladins had entered the Nave, weapons drawn. They held their ground but looked ready to move instantly at the commands of their new masters.

More movement flickered within the sanctum. Kailene could just make out helmed faces and the flashing steel of weapons. They were surrounded. What could she do now?

"An atonement must be made." The Bishop-Prefect now spoke, his voice surprisingly high and sweet, not like his own voice at all. "A reckoning that is long overdue and it starts here."

"Dantol," Aermisiny began. "Why? What possible reason could you have for doing this?"

"No," Bortrum said. "It is not Dantol."

Eleanor gasped at Kailene's side. Bortrum and Aermisiny murmured some warding incantation as Rowt began to snarl, ears flattened against his head. Kailene just stood, watching, her mouth open in astonishment.

The space surrounding the Bishop-Prefect rippled like that of a heat mirage. His body and face... *transformed.*

A Perliox stood before them--a tall, haughty barbarian, adorned with long, jeweled hairlocks, his dark skin scarified with tattooed symbols, a black, floor-length robe clinging to his thin, rangy body. His red eyes burned with an inner fire born of hate and revenge, of that Kailene was certain.

The Animist, she thought, her throat dry. *The one who has caused all of this.* "What have you done with the Bishop-Prefect?" Kailene demanded, her voice coming out stronger than she would have thought.

"Your precious Dantol lies within the sanctum," the Animist answered calmly, his hands moving in strange patterns before him. The motions were fluid and almost hypnotizing, continuously weaving their own kind of dangerous magic. "I took his form and memories and, as such, none could penetrate my disguise. Even you Sacred Ones can be so easily deceived." He shook his head, a disgusted look on his face. "In the end, even before the Set's gates had been breached, Dantol tried to stop me... to stop *us*. 'We are just supposed to take over the Set,' he said. 'There is to be no killing, he said.'" The Animist laughed, a high, keening sound. "How could there not be? Was he such a naïve fool? He helped to plan this. The Olanides must see what they have caused the Perliox to do, what they have caused us to become. It is justice. There can be no justice without loss."

"No!" Bortrum shouted behind Kailene. "Your words lie!"

"It's true," Marcus interjected, his face lit up from within by some fiery light. "Dantol and I have been planning this with the Perliox for the last six moons. The Animist, the Blessed One, needed that much time to work his enchantments against the Set. He needed to subjugate most of the prelates and paladins to his will in order to make this strike successful."

"Lies again!" Bortrum again. "Warding spells were set against the Perliox. And Dantol would not have done such a thing. What you say cannot be!"

"And yet..." the Animist smiled a ghastly smile, one filled with jeweled teeth and malicious intent. "...we are here. Even warding spells fail in time, especially with help." He cast a knowing, sidelong glance at Marcus and then turned his frightening eyes to Kailene. "As for you and your guards, Marshal, it wasn't deemed necessary to take you over. The Bishop-Prefect knew you were young and inexperienced; this was your first watch and he assured us you would fail. You did not even suspect."

"And *yet*," Kailene mocked bitterly. "*We* are here as well. And we have destroyed one of your sky-ships!" She bluffed, not really knowing for certain. The expression on the Animist's face, though, told her she was right.

"It doesn't matter," Marcus said. "Our objective wasn't necessarily to conquer Olan but to send a message; to show that the Perliox will not stand idly by any longer."

"Are you mad?" Aermisiny cried. Her small, sculpted features were reddened with anger. "All this death and carnage for a message? All these innocents killed?"

Marcus bristled. "And what have our people done over the last hundred turnings but persecute such innocents--the Perliox, the native mountain tribes and all those who do not agree with us? Who are not of the same religion? Whose skin is not the same color as ours? Bortrum and you, Marshal! Surely you have experienced such yourselves for being Ofrikane and Gifted? And Thomas with his wings?"

"But we have not killed or brutalized those who mocked us," Bortrum retorted.

"You are still so blind!" Marcus cried. "Don't you remember? Don't you remember what really happened? I thank the Blessed One for opening my eyes, for contacting me through the aether to be a part of this."

"And what of our part in this?" Bortrum demanded. "Why did you bring us here?"

Marcus shook his head. "As well as I know all of you, I still thought the soporific would render you helpless until you could be bound. None of us are as young as we used to be. In that immobilized state, I would have shown you the truth!"

"Still," Bortrum said. "You sent the paladins to kill us."

"No! Only to slow you down. That challenge I knew you would overcome. And now that you are all here, you will see. Just telling you would never have worked--you have to see for yourselves as Dantol and I did."

"We've seen nothing but your treachery!" Aermisiny cried. "You allowed Dantol to be murdered when he realized how wrong you are!"

"There is a higher purpose here that negates..."

Bortrum spat with rage, "Curse you, Marcus! What have you done? You *have* been taken over by this creature."

The Blessed One? Then it is the Animist who must fall! And with him his cursed magic! Making her decision, Kailene cocked her wrist, the forearm dagger clicking into position within its hidden holster. *Rowt,* she thought-sent through her Eye. Marcus had retreated from her mind in order to give his overblown speech; he wouldn't be sensing her thoughts now. *Be ready.*

But the farsenser had sensed *something*--Marcus suddenly turned toward the Animist, his eyes clouded, a look of alarm on his corpulent face. "Blessed One," he said. "There are Imperium troopers approaching the rear gates..."

But the Animist was staring at Kailene, his strange look unsettling. "And you, sister," he said, cocking his head to one side. "How have *you* come to this place?"

Madness, Kailene thought, the bile rising in her throat. *Madness.* She gave a mental signal to Rowt as her arm shot up and outward, releasing the dagger and its poisoned tip toward the Animist.

৪০

BORTRUM

Moving surprisingly fast for one so large, Marcus threw his arm up in front of the Perliox. The farsenser cried out but before Bortrum could see what transpired further, Aermisiny whirled and carried her husband quickly to the side of the altar.

She leaned his broken body between two pillars. "Stay here, my love," Aermisiny said, a sad smile on her lips. "Surely we will remember this Frenten's Eve reunion for the rest of our lives, will we not?"

"No! Aermisiny!" Bortrum watched helplessly as his wife turned back toward the bedlam that had suddenly erupted on the chancel steps. Marcus reeled from the dagger imbedded in his arm, stumbling backwards against the outer wall of the sanctum. The young Marshal and her second took up their swords and prepared to meet the charge of a party of Perliox troopers pouring out of the Holy Sanctum; the hound, Rowt, leaped into the fray, slashing and tearing like a beast risen from the underworld. And Aermisiny...

Bortrum's wife picked up a large, free-standing candelabra, taller by far than even Thomas, and swung it like a club. Several attacking Perliox troopers were sent flying by the makeshift weapon. Aermisiny then flung the candelabra spear-like, into the doorway of the Holy Sanctum, blocking its passage.

The paladins at the front of the Nave began converging on the altar. The Animist sidestepped the melee and walked from the altar toward them, hoping, no doubt, for their greater numbers to protect him. And yet, his calm gait bespoke a supreme overconfidence.

Or perhaps an ultimate resignation?

"Watch out!" Bortrum cried as one of the troopers swung a mace at Aermisiny. He threw a crutch at the enemy, his frustration exploding within him. How he hated his useless body at this moment! He wanted to help, not just stand here and watch! At the Battle of Olan, he had been the First Healer, curing those wounded in battle. But now, he felt so helpless. If only he could move and walk like he did in his dreams!

A Gift? More like a curse!

Kailene and Eleanor were fully engaged now. The Knight-Wardens circled and fought back-to-back as their swords cut a swath of blood among the Perliox. The hound seemed to have struck a superstitious chord within the enemy, causing the attacking troopers to retreat from him in fear. But the Marshal and her comrades were outnumbered. It was only a matter of time.

The Animist passed a few hands reach from him, giving Bortrum a sneering glance as if he was nothing more than an insect, too insignificant to bother with. Bortrum pushed himself forward and, straining his good arm, grasped the Perliox by the collar of his robe.

He pulled himself to the Animist's back, wrapping his arm around the Perliox's neck. "Monster!" he cried into the Animist's ear, tightening his grip as his left arm dragged the bound crutch behind him. "Evil savage!"

The Animist reached up and peeled Bortrum from him as if the Gifted One were an insect. He pushed him to the floor, kneeling over him like some creature out of nightmare. His breath smelled like scented fruit. This had happened to Bortrum before. Would Thomas be able to save him now as he had that day so long ago?

"If we are savages," the Animist whispered. "It is because you made us so. Your kind came to our lands to kill and plunder. Unsuspecting fools that we were, we welcomed you with open arms."

Bortrum struggled, fear giving way to rage. "Liar!

Your people deceived and attacked us just as you have done now!"

"We defended ourselves then." The Animist released Bortrum and stood over him. "And we do the same now. You were so blinded to your own greed and lust for power that you couldn't see the wrong you did in the name of your 'Almighty One.' And now we resort to your own methods of deceit and violence to reclaim that which is ours. That is how far *we* have fallen."

Bortrum saw the paladins rush by on either side of him and the Animist, heading for the altar. *Too many,* he thought. *There are too many.*

The Animist knelt down again and stretched out his hand...

ଔ

KAILENE

"Ugh!" Kailene stumbled backwards as one of the Perliox booted her in the stomach. The pen-rae was winding down, its energy diminishing for both her and Eleanor. The young Marshal hurt in several parts of her body; her breath came short and hard; her arms felt heavy; she bled from a number of small wounds.

Eleanor fared no better though Kailene's second fought like a wild woman against the enemy. The small Gifted One called Aermisiny picked up a trooper five times her size over her head and threw him against the wall. Rowt harassed and harried several of the enemy, spittle and blood flying from his ravaging jaws.

Kailene fought back, pressing against two of the Perliox. She almost stumbled over the still-twitching body of the traitor, Marcus. Her quick glance caught the scene in front of the chancel steps--the Animist bending over Bortrum as the bespelled paladins charged the altar.

She barely ducked under a sweeping blow by one of her opponents as she pulled the dagger from the farsenser's quivering flesh. It's poison would be greatly reduced now but the blade itself would still be effective.

Sacred Seven, she thought. *Though you are not*

who we thought you were--guide my hand now! She
threw the blood-stained blade through the throng of
troopers and paladins like thread through the eye of a
needle.

Kailene felt something hit her from behind. She
fell forward, her back bursting with pain. Another
trooper struck her a glancing blow with his sword in the
head, knocking her down the chancel steps.

"Kai!" Eleanor screamed. Somewhere in the
distance, Rowt howled. Kailene fell but saw the Animist
stumbling past the fallen Bortrum toward the Nave's
entrance, the dagger protruding from the Perliox's back.

Cries of agony sounded all around her. The
paladins began dropping their weapons, clutching their
heads and bellies as if they were on fire. With the
Animist mortally wounded, his magic began leaving
them, the spell-sickness taking over. Some of the Perliox
troopers began fleeing in every direction, their focus
scattered.

Kailene crawled toward Bortrum, blood flowing
from her two new wounds. Eleanor was at her back then,
defending her from the remaining Perliox. Aermisiny
rushed past her to her husband's side.

The Animist turned back towards the altar, his

face lit up with some emotion--Ecstasy? Victory? Acceptance? He fell to his knees and raised his shaking hands toward the ceiling dome of the Pantocrator. There was something...

At that moment, from the front of the Nave, Olanide troopers with the sigil of Fort Pennit inscribed on their uniforms burst in. The Animist cried out in some unknown language. Flashes of blue light erupted from his eyes and fingertips; his body trembled and glowed...

A noise like scraping metal filled the chamber. The massive windows on each side of the Nave ballooned inward... and exploded. Shards of thick glass were blown into the Nave's interior like hundreds of crossbow bolts. Kailene screamed, reaching backwards toward Eleanor when something wet and powerful grasped her by the arm and pulled.

Rowt dragged his mistress into the shelter of an overhanging statue, the sculpted figure's cloak spread wide. Kailene gasped at the pain of her wounds, hearing the screams of the troopers and the remaining Perliox.

Sharpened, shattered glass fell around them like a storm of sparkling, ragged death.

Rowt! My strong boy! My beautiful boy! Rowt

nuzzled her with his bloody nose, whining softly. His despair filled her Eye. *Help me... help me to my feet.*

But even as the last of the glass fell, dancing like glittering diamonds as it bounced on the floor, Kailene could see the results of the Animist's magic. Leaning on Rowt, Kailene kicked the shards away from the hound's bare paws and shuffled to where Eleanor lay on her back. A piece of glass lodged in her friend's throat, her once-beautiful green eyes staring lifelessly, her blood soaking the red carpet with an even brighter crimson stain.

"El...Eleanor," Kailene gasped, kneeling painfully at her second's side. "No, no, my lovely girl. No..." Tears flowed uncontrollably down her cheeks, a searing pain of heartbreak burned in her chest. She moaned, rocking back and forth as she held tightly onto the lifeless husk that once was Eleanor.

This wasn't supposed to happen. Everything had gone wrong. Everything.

A sound brought Kailene back--a groan sounded from her right. There, Kailene saw Aermisiny, her tiny body covering her husband's to protect him from the falling glass. Beyond her, the Animist lay like a tailor's pin cushion--pierced with a score of deadly glass projectiles. But the sound had not issued from the so-called Blessed One or the small Sacred One--Aermisiny too lay dead from several shard wounds.

It had to be Bortrum.

Kailene crawled to the where the two old ones' bodies lay, not caring that the glass cut her hands and knees. She was beyond pain now. Everything had gone wrong. So much death.

"All for a lie," Bortrum whispered as if reading her thoughts. "All this for a lie." The Ofrikane held his wife's body with his one hand, clinging to it with a grip of iron.

"The reinforcements from Fort Pennit are here," Kailene said through her tears. "They will help you."

Bortrum shook his head. "No," he said. "It is too late for me. Aermisiny is dead and all my perceptions, all the reasons I have had for living my life, have blown away in this wind of blood and death. The Animist, as Dantol, told me we had to right a great wrong. He was right, he was right. Why hadn't Wing-Ma seen this? His gift was so unpredictable."

"Don't try to talk, noble lord."

Bortrum snorted, his mouth bubbling with bloody froth. "Noble? No, sister. Not so. I... I am sorry for your friend, Eleanor. She was a brave soul but she too died for all the wrong reasons."

Kailene felt dizzy. The blood from her wounds was making her light-headed. She was having difficulty breathing. "What... what do you mean?"

Bortrum breathed hard; his eyes seemed unfocused. "The Animist. He touched me with his magic and showed me. What Marcus said was true. We were the monsters. Not them. Those of us who came to settle this land so long ago thought we were so much the mightier, so much more superior. We took everything that we wanted. We destroyed the Perliox way of life because they were in our way. We took Set Perl, their last stronghold, for our own. This Set..."

Kailene's vision swam. "No," she said. "The Animist magicked you. That is not what happened. The history scrolls..."

"Not so. My Gift would reject such magic laid against me. What the Animist revealed to me was the truth. The scrolls lie, written by the conquerors. Marcus never felt as joyous after the exile of the Perliox as the rest of us did. He never relished our victory. He suspected the true events even then and so was ripe for the Animist's influence. He brought all of us here for this reunion... not to kill us but to show us... to..."

Suddenly, Bortrum reached out and grabbed Kailene's braid, pulling her face close to his with surprising strength. "I will open your Eye," he rasped, pressing his forehead to hers. "I will cure you of your ignorance."

಄

KAILENE

Kailene stood on what remained of Set Olan's siege wall, looking down at the shattered city. Troopers, Knight-Wardens and relief workers from Fort Pennit and surrounding outposts had poured into Olan to help. Aid stations and food lines had been set up all over the city and within the Set. The Fort's strange, motorized conveyances that had brought reinforcements so quickly rumbled through the streets, dropping off supplies and men.

Thankfully, the Galan-Hai delegates, except for their ceremonial hostage, were unharmed. They too joined in to render assistance, pledging to avenge this atrocity and going so far as to promise to join with the Shawn-Ryn to work together toward that goal. A common enemy made for strange allies, it seemed.

At least some small good has come out of this horror then. Kailene closed her eyes, her heart breaking. Bortrum had healed her again at the end, curing her wounds a second time yet giving her another, more painful one in return. He had passed the visions of the Perliox Animist on to her--the "truth" of their place in this world.

We were the enemy, she thought, her heart heavy with more than grief. *Not just the Olanides but all of us. We always were. By saying and doing nothing, we allowed such evil to come to pass. To be forgotten.*

"Use this knowledge to right this horrible wrong!" the dying Bortrum had pleaded with her. "I beg you, find our children, mine and Aermisiny's and Marcus'. They too are Gifted. They can help you..."

And one other, Kailene thought, remembering what the beautiful Solana had told her about her and Thomas' son. *At Set Xalatar.*

Below, in the ravaged courtyard, the body of Eleanor and the remains of her other guards were being wrapped in makeshift shrouds and loaded onto packhorses. She would accompany them back to their prefecture for burial. Ayo had been found by some of the troopers of Fort Pennit--he too would be given the proper respect in his native soil.

Yet it wouldn't be respect Kailene would be facing when she returned. It would be judgment. She had failed her first watch and that failure had cost so many their lives. The Council of Knight-Wardens would not be lenient.

Still, not all had perished. Solana's body had

vanished from Fort Pennit, Kailene had been told. Some of the inhabitants there said they saw a winged figure carrying her away. *I hope they survived,* she thought hopefully. *I would be glad if some of the Seven did.*

She knelt at Rowt's side. "Is it all true, my strong boy?" she asked, more to the wind than to her hound. Tears ran down her cheeks. Rowt whined and nuzzled her neck. "Is what the Animist passed on to me through Bortrum what really happened? Is it really the truth?"

She had to find out. Kailene burned with a desire to set things right. Even now runners and homing-fowl were being sent out to the surrounding Sets throughout Glimmerlaan prefecture. The Perliox would be hunted down although Kailene was certain they were dissipating throughout the countryside, perhaps preparing for a long hit-and-run war.

A war they may have every right to wage. She descended the steps with Rowt right behind her. *Yet, in the end, they did not opt for peace or understanding any more than we did.*

After the funeral and cremation rituals she would throw herself at the mercy of the Council. She would try to convince them there was a way to atone for this catastrophe, to tell them of her plan--to set out to find the children of the Gifted Ones as Bortrum had so desperately pleaded. It seemed a far-fetched idea but it was the only one Kailene had. Perhaps, together she and the Seven's offspring could find the truth and a way to make peace--once and for all.

Bortrum told me he and Aermisiny had two children, Kailene thought, remembering again. *Marcus had two, Thomas and Solana had the one. Along with me and Rowt, perhaps we could make up a new Sacred Seven. But this time for all the right reasons.*

She mounted her horse at the head of the funeral column. Rowt prowled impatiently, eager to be off. Several troopers from Fort Pennit would be accompanying Kailene. Ironically, it was a beautiful fall day on the aftermath of so much death--the sun shone brilliantly in a cloudless sky.

One last thought lingered in Kailene's mind. Like a rabid hound prowling at the edges of her thoughts, it refused to go away. The Perliox trooper Rowt had killed and the Animist--both acted as if they knew her somehow. "Sister" he had called her. As if she were a Perliox herself.

Impossible, she thought, finally banishing that insane idea to the dark recesses of her mind. *Impossible.*

With a heavy sigh, Kailene turned one last time to look at Set Olan and then coaxed her mount forward, urging him home.

ॐ

EPILOGUE

Set Perl

The Cycle of Merat ~

Forty Turnings Before

Ferendel the Animist entered the dirty prison cell beneath Set Perl. She walked straight to the captive, knowing there wasn't much time. The Olanides had overrun and taken the Set. Many of her fellow magickers had been killed. The rest were on the run. It was only a matter of time before the enemy discovered the tunnel system constructed beneath the citadel and flushed her and the others of her kind into the open. *I must get an answer from this so-called Gifted One!* she thought. *Even I and my brother and sister Animists don't possess the power to see the future as he does.*

She knelt before the prisoner, grunting at the pain in her body. She removed her helm and let out a long, quavering sigh as her single, dark braid tumbled down her back. Ferendel had been wounded in the battle with the Olanides and now nursed an injured thigh and shoulder. Bandages and makeshift stitches beneath her armor kept the bleeding to a trickle but the pain was more than evident. That was nothing compared to the prisoner's suffering; that was why Ferendel refused to use her magic to treat herself. She must save all of her power for the poor wretch in front of her since her superiors would not allow an enemy to be treated. They had refused to listen to her plea that there was more at stake here than just one person's pain.

The torches inset into the wall niches of the cell revealed a sorry sight. Blind and broken, the Gifted One called Wing-Ma lay crumpled in a corner of the cell, his white tunic and trousers covered in blood and filth and smelling of urine. The seer had been captured at one of the enemy's command tents and mortally wounded in the process. If Ferendel hadn't recognized the Gifted One and intervened, the Perliox troopers would have killed him as they killed the others. *I must know what he knows!* the Animist thought as she waved her hand over Wing-Ma to work her restorative magic.

The copper-skinned Gifted One stirred, his features softening momentarily into relief. But his eyes... though only dark recesses in the seer's face, there was power reflected there. A cold shiver ran through Ferendel.

"Ah," Wing-Ma breathed, his voice a ragged whisper. "I see that you are the one."

What? "Gifted One," Ferendel said, trying to rein in her impatience. "We have no time for riddles and word games. I regret your suffering but you must tell me how we can save this day. Tell me how we can make peace. We Perliox are not the demons you envision. We have been unjustly persecuted."

"I know that now, too late, to my dishonor and shame." Wing-Ma coughed, spitting up blood. A crooked smile creased his lined features. He was the oldest of the Seven, Ferendel knew. Older by far than the others--their leader, perhaps? He certainly hadn't seemed to be afraid as he used his Gift to predict when and where the Perliox would position their troopers during the battle. No doubt he had foreseen this captivity. If so, why hadn't he avoided being taken?

"I had to speak with you," the seer said as if reading her thoughts. "There was no other way. I had to let events play out. I had to speak with the one who would save me at the command tent. You are the one..."

"Speak to me then!" Ferendel cried, flinching at the pain in her shoulder. "Tell me..."

"This day cannot be saved," Wing-Ma quickly replied. "But the future can. I cannot see everything; my sight is limited. I did not realize the one I needed to speak to at the end would be a Perliox nor that I would be lying here under Set Perl in such a state but here we are."

"And?" Ferendel was beginning to regret this. She had helped organize several peace conferences with the Olanides but to no avail. In the end, there was too much dark history between the two races, too much hate and too much blood spilled. Both sides wanted war and she had been forced by duty and obligation to do battle herself.

And now their ancient stronghold had been taken.

But surely, there was still hope. She had never been the only one to think so. But was this feeling she had that this blind man could help simply desperation on her part?

She had seen friends and comrades killed. She had witnessed the beginning of the end of the Perliox way of life. The Animists' magic had not been strong enough to overcome that of the Olanides' Priest-Mages and the First Paladin's sky-ships. Her lover and fellow Animist had been brought down by the Gifted winged one. Was it indeed too late for all of them?

"The circle must be completed," the seer continued, his voice thick with pain and emotion. "Although it is more like a wandering, tangled trail. Your people will be driven into the mountains and contained for many turnings by guarding spells and powerful magic. But you, and you alone, must go south instead. There... there is a way and there is still time for you to escape."

"South?" Ferendel felt her last hopes fading. This sounded no better than any fortune-teller would relate.

"Yes. To Atmium prefecture. Fifteen turnings from now, you will give birth to the child that will help save the future for all our peoples. The father will be an Ofrikane..."

"You are mad," the Animist spat. "The Ofrikanes hate us as much as the Olanides."

"Yes, but this union is foreseen." The seer began another bout of coughing, his body wracked with spasms. Ferendel ran her hand over and through his aura, calming him further but she knew time was running out.

"Thank... thank you," Wing-Ma gasped. The torches cast flickering shadows across his tortured face. "I tell you only what I see. You will bear the child of an Ofrikane Beastmaster and then, after the child's birth, you will leave both it and the father so it may be mothered by another. Never have my visions been so clear."

"I would never abandon a child! You lie..."

Wing-Ma weakly shook his head. "There are many future paths, many branches that can be taken depending on a decision here, a choice there. This is the only one that will bring the peace you desire though it will be long and painful and may not happen in your lifetime. There will be much suffering. But it will set in motion those events that will bring about the future you seek. You must take the opportunity." A pause. And then, "For the sake of all our children."

The Gifted seer sighed and lay his head back against the hard, cold wall of his prison. "If you really believe, you... you must take it." And then he spoke no more.

Ferendel stood and stared down upon the body of the blind man. *Madness,* she thought, trying to calm the racing of her heart. *We are all doomed.* She turned at a sound behind her. One of her guard stood in the cell's entrance.

"My Lady," he said with a bow. "The enemy has found the tunnels' access. We need to get out at once."

"Yes," she murmured, once more looking at the dead seer. "You go on ahead. I'll catch up in a moment."

Ferendel paused. *A child,* she thought in sudden

wonder. *One who will help to change everything. I pray it is true.* It seemed her decision had already been made, despite her reservation. *Very well, Gifted One,* she thought, knowing that, in the end, her people had nothing without hope. And hope had been the only thing that had kept her going. *I'll do it your way.* She grasped a torch off the wall and ran into the corridor.

Watching her trooper disappear at the far end of the tunnel, Ferendel the Animist took a deep breath and set off in the opposite direction--toward the tunnel's rear egress that led to the south.

And her new life.

୫୬

THE END

Read more of Larry's
short fiction on
his web site:
http://mysite.verizon.net/vzesw7nb/

THE SIXTH PRECEPT is

available in print and ebook formats at:
http://www.amazon.com/The-Sixth-
Precept-Larry-Ivkovich/dp/0615554245

It's companion short story ebook, **A
CONCERNED CITIZEN**, is available at:
http://www.amazon.com/Concerned-
CItizen-Publishing-Chap-eBook-
ebook/dp/B008POR5RO

Made in the USA
Charleston, SC
20 May 2013